Elfangor's Journey

the andalite
chronicles

Elfangor's Journey

the andalite chronicles

K.A. Applegate

AN
APPLE
PAPERBACK

SCHOLASTIC INC.
New York Toronto London Auckland Sydney

ISBN 0-590-10879-4

10 9 8 7 6 5 4 3

Printed in the U.S.A.   40

First Scholastic printing, September 1997

For Jean Feiwel

And, as always, for Michael

Elfangor's Journey

the
andalite
chronicles

Prologue

My name is Elfangor.

I am an Andalite prince. And I am about to die.

My fighter is damaged. I have crash-landed on the surface of the planet called Earth. I believe that my great Dome ship has been destroyed. I fear that my little brother Aximili is already dead.

We did not expect the Yeerks to be here in such force. We made a mistake. We underestimated the Yeerks. Not for the first time. We would have defeated their Pool ship and its fighters. But there was a Blade ship in orbit as well.

The Blade ship of Visser Three.

Two Yeerk Bug fighters are landing on either side of me now. The abomination Visser Three is here as well. I can feel him. I can sense his evil.

I cannot defeat the visser in one-on-one combat. I am weak from my injuries. Too weak to morph. Too weak to fight.

This is my *hirac delest* — my final statement. I have formed the mental link to the thought-speak transponder in my fighter's computer. I will record my memories before the Yeerks annihilate all trace of me.

If this message someday reaches the Andalite world, I want the truth to be known. I am called a great warrior. A hero. But there is a great deal that no Andalite knows about me. I have not lied, but I have kept the truth a secret.

This is not my first visit to Earth. I spent many years on Earth . . . and yet, no time at all.

I landed here now in this construction site because I was looking for a great weapon: the Time Matrix. The existence of this weapon is also a secret.

So many secrets in my life . . . mistakes. Things I should have done. All the strands of my strange life seem to be coming together. It all seems inevitable now. Of course my death would come on Earth. Of course the child would be here. Of course it would be Visser Three who would take my life.

I am too weak to locate the Time ship now. I will die here. But I have left a legacy. Visser Three thinks he has won our long, private war. But I've left a little surprise behind.

I have given the morphing power to five human youths.

I know that in doing this I have broken Andalite law. I know that this action will be condemned by all my people. But the Yeerks are here on Earth. Visser Three is here. The humans must be given a chance to resist. The human race cannot fall to the Yeerks the way the Hork-Bajir race did.

I have given the morphing power to five young humans. Children, really. But sometimes children can accomplish amazing things.

I have no choice but to hope. Because it was I who created Visser Three. I who caused the abomination. I cannot go peacefully to my death, knowing that I created the creature who will enslave the human race.

I came to this place, this empty construction site, looking for the weapon I know is hidden here. But there is no time now. No time . . .

The visser is here. He is laughing at my weakness. He is savoring his victory over me.

This is the *hirac delest* of Elfangor-Sirinial-Shamtul, Andalite prince. I open my mind in the ritual of death. I open my mind and let all my memories — all my secrets — go to be recorded by the computer.

This is not just a message to my own people. I hope that someday humans will read it as well. Because humans are also my people. Loren . . . and the boy I have just met, but not for the first time. . . .

chapter 1

Twenty-one years before . . .

The Yeerks were loose. Like some terrifying disease, they spread their evil from planet to planet. They took species after species. They crushed all resistance.

Their spiderlike Pool ships roamed throughout the galaxy. Their armies of Taxxons and Hork-Bajir, all under the control of Yeerk slugs, rampaged — killing, butchering, enslaving.

They were annihilating entire planets.

Only we Andalites stood against them. But we had been caught off-guard. Our mighty Dome ships, each more than a match for anything the Yeerks had, were spread too thin. Our spies, even though they used top-secret Andalite morphing technology, were unable to penetrate Yeerk secrets. For five years our princes had fought the vissers of the Yeerk Empire. They said the war could go on for another fifty years . . . another hundred years.

We were outnumbered. We had fought many battles and lost too many of them. But arrogant as I was, I was confident that if only I could get into the fight, I could make a difference.

I, Elfangor, was going to become a great warrior, a prince, a hero.

I was posted as an *aristh,* a cadet, to the Dome ship *StarSword.* But so far, after six months in space looking for an elusive Yeerk task force, I had not exactly proven myself to be a great hero.

In fact, I had proven myself to be a clumsy, slow-witted, and quite possibly hopeless fool. At least, according to my instructors.

<*Aristh* Elfangor! How many times do I have to tell you: The killing blow should be as graceful as it is fast!> Sofor yelled his thought-speak loudly enough that half the ship probably heard him.

I stood facing him, trying to stand light and easy on my four hooves, just like I was supposed to. At the same time I had to think about where my weight was centered, and whether the tilt of my upper body signaled when I was going to strike, and whether the grass floor under my hooves was uneven, and whether my hands were out of the way, and about a million other things a warrior should know for tail-fighting.

Sofor was bigger than me. He was a full warrior, while I was just a lowly *aristh* — a warrior-cadet. If this had been an actual battle, Sofor would have sliced me up twenty different ways in less than a second.

Maybe. Sometimes I thought I'd be faster and better if it was a real battle, not just a lesson. I was sure if my life depended on it, I could win.

In any case, Sofor was not my enemy. He was my teacher.

<Watch my eyes, not my tail,> Sofor said. <My main eyes, you nitwit, not my stalk eyes! Keep your main eyes on mine, your stalk eyes on my tail.>

I watched his main eyes, but it wasn't easy. His left eye had a huge scar running right beneath it. I tried to focus all my thoughts down to nothingness, just like Sofor had taught me.

<Your mind will never know when it is time to strike. Only your *instinct* can guide you,> he reminded me.

Suddenly . . . FWAPPP!

I fired the muscles in my tail! The bladed tip cracked the air, it moved so fast. I could barely see my own tail as it struck.

The blade arched over my head toward Sofor's face, and I thought, *Hey, maybe old Sofar will end up with a new scar.* If I landed a blow on Sofor, I'd be a hero with every poor *aristh* who had ever suffered under him.

Then . . . SWOOP! FWAPP! FWAPP! FWAPP!

Sofor blocked my tail blade with his tail, turned it aside, and in about a tenth of a second delivered three lightning blows. One to each side of my head, and a third that left his razor-sharp tail blade pressed right up against my throat. The blows stopped just a hair from cutting my skin.

If Sofor so much as twitched, he could remove my head from my shoulders.

<Not bad, *Aristh* Elfangor,> Sofor said with a laugh. <Not bad at all. That strike of yours could almost have hit me . . . if I were asleep!>

He laughed again and pulled his tail away. <Remember, don't think about it, do it. You're too intellectual. You think too much. You should be a scientist, not a warrior. There's no time for thought in a fight. There is only time for your training to join with your instinct.>

<I guess even you must have forgotten that once,> I muttered.

I regretted the words the instant they were out of my head.

Sofor turned his stalk eyes toward me. He had a dangerous expression. <What did you say, *Aristh*?>

<Nothing . . . just . . . um, nothing,> I stammered. But I was staring at the scar below his eye the whole time.

<Ah, I see. You've noticed my little scar. Yes, quite a nasty cut. Know how I got it?>

I shook my head. What was I doing, getting smart with Sofor? What was the matter with me? Was I insane?

<I got this scar from my own teacher. He wasn't as sweet and understanding as I am. He didn't like uppity *arisths*.>

The old warrior laughed at his own wit, turned away, and went galloping off across the grass, holding his tail as high as an Andalite half his age would.

I breathed a huge sigh of relief. I looked around the dome to see whether anyone else was watching me be humiliated. The dome of a Dome ship is a circular area about a third of a mile across. It is filled with grass, trees, ground rushes, and flowers. There is a lake in the middle and a stream that runs around the circumference.

It's as much like home as it can be. You'd almost think you were running across any well-kept area on the home world. But when you look up, you see that you are in space, protected only by a clear plastic bubble, a dome.

I saw other warriors off running across the grass, feeding and playing and practicing their skills. But none seemed to be watching me.

I replayed the fight with Sofor. How had he known the exact second when I would strike? What had given me away?

What was the matter with me? Was I actually mad because Sofor was faster than me? Of *course* he was a better fighter than me. He'd been in more battles than I could imagine.

But it still made me angry. I didn't like people laughing at me. And I didn't like losing.

Through my stalk eyes I saw someone coming up behind me. He'd been hidden by a stand of trees. I recognized him immediately, of course: Arbron. We were the only two *ariths.*

Great. More bad news. I didn't really like Arbron much. He was very competitive with me. And still he never seemed to take anything seriously.

<Well, hello, Elfangor,> he said. <Having fun with the old Yeerk-killer?>

<Hello, *Aristh* Arbron,> I said, so stiffly I sounded like my own father. <I don't think it's very respectful to refer to Sofor as the old Yeerk-killer. He is a full warrior, after all, and our personal combat instructor.>

Now Arbron laughed at me. <Yeah, right, Elfangor. Like you're so respectful. Teach me to be as respectful as you, *pleeeease.* >

He laughed again, and I was starting to get even angrier. It was bad enough having Sofor laugh at me. At least he outranked me. But Arbron was just a lowly *aristh* like me. Lowlier, because I had four days seniority over him.

<This is a Dome ship, not a play field,> I said.

Arbron kicked lightly at the grass with one hoof in a gesture of contempt. Then he said the insult that went with the gesture. <Elfangor, when are you going to get your hooves back on the grass and out of the air?>

<Some of us actually care about being better fighters. The people need us. These are evil times.>

Arbron laughed. <You don't fool me. You're not some mighty prince or hero. You're just another scared, confused *aristh* on his first big deep-space mission. And by the way, you shift weight to your left hind leg when you get ready to strike. That's how old Sofor knew.>

I was getting ready to say something really crushing to Arbron, but just then there came an announcement. It was a direct-beamed thought-speak summons.

<*Arisths* Elfangor and Arbron to the battle bridge.>

I stared at Arbron. He stared at me. We were both frozen in place. Our argument was totally forgotten because we were both busy being shocked and horrified.

See, it was *impossible*. Neither of us had ever been to the battle bridge. The battle bridge was where the captain was. And the captain of a Dome ship is like one of the ancient gods. I mean, captains don't even *look* at *arisths*.

<What did we do?> Arbron asked anxiously.

<I don't know,> I moaned, <but it must have been really out of line.>

<We're in trouble. We are in definite trouble,> Arbron said.

chapter 2

A Dome ship is built with the dome at one end and then, far away, far back, there are the three huge engines. Zero-space engines, and you probably know how powerful those are. Connecting the dome to the engines is a long, long shaft. Inside this shaft is the place where everyone has their quarters — their private areas.

For *arisths,* the quarters are tiny. I mean, extremely tiny. If you want to turn around you have to back out into the hallway. In my quarters I have holograms of my father and mother, of course. Plus a wish-flower representing the little brother I'll be getting in a few years. The Electorate has voted to allow more children to be born since we're in a war now. They say if the war goes on for long and there are lots of battle deaths, some families may even have three and four children.

Personally, I don't think it will come to that. And even having one sibling is bad enough. Now, in addition to the morning ritual and the evening ritual, I have to do the wish-flower ritual. And you have to do the wish-flower ritual at the wish-flower, of course, which is in my tiny quarters. And you can imagine how impossible that is!

My entire back half sticks out into the hallway and people are jostling past while I'm chanting, <We welcome our hopes embodied, we welcome a new branch of the tree, we welcome . . .> So on and so on.

It's not easy being an *aristh*. Naturally, warriors and princes get bigger quarters. And of course the captain has quarters so big he can practically play driftball in there.

But the captain isn't usually in his quarters. He's usually on the battle bridge. That's where Arbron and I were heading, as fast as our hooves could carry us down the long central shaft.

<We're dead,> I said. <There's no way the captain calls us to the bridge unless we are in huge trouble.>

<Maybe it's something good,> Arbron suggested. <Maybe he wants to tell us we're doing well in our studies.>

<Yeah. Right. Or maybe he wants our advice,> I suggested sarcastically. <Captain Feyorn, the hero of like a thousand space battles, probably wants the advice of a pair of *arisths*.>

All the while we were running. Running past the closed doors of various private quarters and storerooms and plasma conduits. Our hooves clicked on the hard, rough-textured floor. A prince stepped out of his quarters and I practically ran him down.

<Sorry!> I yelled. <We've been called to the battle bridge!>

The prince rolled his eyes and shook his head. But he knew: When the captain calls, you don't waste time.

As we neared the battle bridge we saw more and more people in the hall. We weren't the only ones heading there. And then I started to notice some fighter pilots moving off toward the fighter bays.

You can always tell a fighter pilot. There's a swagger they have. It's almost like there's a special light that seems to shine on them.

When I'm a full warrior I'm going to be a fighter pilot.

<There's going to be a battle!> Arbron said.

<Yeerks!> I said. <We're going to burn some Yeerks!> I hoped I sounded tough and fierce.

We barreled into the battle bridge just as the tactical officer, Prince Nescord, bellowed, <Where in a dark sun are those two *arisths*?>

<Right here, sir!> I said.

<Here, sir!> Arbron echoed.

The tactical officer — the T.O. — looked at us like we might be a couple of pieces of dung stuck to his hoof. Then he turned to the captain. <Captain, the two *arisths* are here.>

Of course the captain already knew we were there. They say Captain Feyorn can practically see through walls. He knows everything that goes on aboard his ship.

He stood in the center of the room, with the T.O. on his right and Prince Breeyar, commander of all fighter squadrons, on his left.

The room was circular, with bright monitors glowing and computer screens reeling off data. Holographic monitors created images in midair, and there were sound-speech info-tags and thought-speech computer warnings.

Warriors working on the battle bridge often used hand signals between themselves so that the thought-speak noise wouldn't become a jumble.

At the front of the battle bridge was a large, holographic image showing the space around us. We were in normal space, not Zero-space, so the background was black, filled with bright stars.

<Magnify,> the T.O. said.

The hologram of space grew more detailed. Suddenly it was as if actual stars, each as big as my fist, were hovering inside the battle bridge.

<Isolate the target and magnify,> the tactical officer said.

Now the hologram showed just a slice of a single

star. It was an average yellow star. I glanced up at the readout above the hologram. It showed that the star had nine planets, gas giants on the outer edge, smaller planets in tighter orbit. The sixth planet was front and center in the display. It had a rather beautiful set of rings.

<There he is,> Prince Breeyar said. He was very calm, but you could tell he was a predator looking at prey.

I searched the hologram of space for a clue. Then I saw it: a tiny, bright point that was moving against the background of the ringed planet.

Was it a Yeerk ship?

<I think we have a Skrit Na raider,> the captain said.

<Yes, Captain,> the T.O. agreed. <He's accelerating. He'll be able to go to Zero-space in twenty minutes. Sensors show he came from the third planet in this system.>

<On-screen,> Captain Feyorn said.

Suddenly the hologram shifted and we were looking at a small planet with a single large moon. The planet was blue with swirls of white, and land masses that were brown and green.

<What do we have on this planet?>

<There is a sentient species there. They have achieved orbital space flight and have landed on their moon. Sensors show presence of nuclear

weapons. And we're picking up transmissions in various parts of the electromagnetic spectrum. All in all, probably a Level Six civilization. I would recommend —>

The captain cut him off by raising one finger on one hand. Then the captain turned his head and his main eyes toward Arbron and me.

He looked right at me. Right at *me*. I felt my blood turn to sludge and my brain grind to a halt.

<Tell me, *Aristh*, the situation: We have a Skrit Na raider leaving a Level Six civilization. Twenty minutes till he's safe in Zero-space. What do you recommend?>

No, this wasn't happening. The captain really *was* asking my advice. Clearly I was dreaming.

<What do I recommend?> I asked, feeling the knife-edge of panic. <Um . . . um, dispatch fighters on an intercept course?>

<Is that a question or a statement?> the captain asked.

I sucked in air and tried not to faint. <Dispatch fighters for an intercept. Send two on an intercept course, and bring two up behind on a chase vector.>

<And you,> the captain said, turning his awful gaze on Arbron. <What do we do when we intercept? And why?>

<The Skrit Na are smugglers and renegades. And

they sometimes serve the Yeerks. So we board the Skrit Na ship and check for any violations.> He said it perfectly. Like he had rehearsed.

Then he blew it. <And if they put up a fight, we put some tail into them!>

The captain, the prince, the T.O., every warrior on the bridge, and I all stared at Arbron like he was insane. Which he obviously was. You don't say <put some tail into them> to the captain! That's something you say in a schoolyard fight.

The captain looked at Prince Breeyar and the tactical officer. He shrugged. <I guess we'd better do what the two *arisths* say, eh? The big one looks like he's ready to faint. And the other one thinks he's *you*, Breeyar.>

That got a laugh from everyone on the bridge.

<Launch fighters,> the captain said. <Oh, and those Skrit Na ships are so cramped inside we'd better send along a couple of our people who can move around in there. Now. Who do we have that's small enough to fit inside a Skrit Na freighter?>

Suddenly, I realized that everyone on the battle bridge was looking at me and Arbron. And then I realized we were both younger and smaller than anyone else.

And that's when I almost did faint.

The captain was going to send us into battle.

chapter 3

<Okay, who takes the helm, and who takes weapons?> Arbron asked.

<I have four days of seniority over you,> I said coolly. <I take the helm.>

I could see that he wanted to argue. He wanted to fly the fighter, of course. But there was no chance I was going to miss out on flying my first combat mission. No chance. And I *did* have seniority.

<Okay,> Arbron said coldly. <You fly it. I'll shoot. Not that we'll be doing any shooting.>

The inside of a fighter is not exactly roomy. This was an older model, built for two, but it was still not exactly big.

<Figures they'd give us an old piece of junk Model Fourteen to fly,> I said, staring at the controls as if I'd never seen them before.

<What did you expect them to give us? A brand-new Model Twenty-two?>

For a second I forgot that this was my first official combat command. I shot a glance at Arbron, and the two of us almost burst out laughing.

<This is great,> I said.

<I just wish it was Yeerks, not some old Skrit Na,> Arbron said.

I closed my main eyes, leaving only my stalk eyes open. I wanted to focus. I had been trained on fighters, of course. I was pretty good as a pilot. But still, I was going to be flying alongside Prince Breeyar in his personal squadron. Everyone in the squadron was a great fighter pilot. And Breeyar could just about fly a fighter through a black hole and back out again.

I deeply did not want anything to go wrong. The thought of how humiliated I'd be if I missed a turn or something was too awful to think about.

<Power up,> I told the ship's systems. <Prepare for launch.>

You could feel the old fighter come alive. The monitors glowed. The floor hummed and vibrated up through my legs. I touched a screen with my fingers and the viewport became transparent. We could see directly out now, through an actual window, not just a screen. Of course we were still in the fighter bay inside the Dome ship, so there wasn't anything to see.

<Automatic launch sequence begins in ten seconds,> the prince called. <Simultaneous drop. Go to burn on my mark. Acceleration standard.>

<Weapons powered,> Arbron told me.

17

<Five seconds to launch,> the computer said.

<Please don't let me screw this up,> I prayed. I thought I'd said it silently till I noticed Arbron nodding in agreement.

<Two seconds,> the computer prompted.

<Hold on,> I said.

FWOOOOOSH!

We were blown out the hatch, out into black space. Ahead of us, four other fighters, all Model 22s, dropped from the bottom of the Dome ship's fighter bay.

<Intercept team, go to burn,> the prince said with total calm.

Two of the fighters lit up their engines. With a brilliant blue glow, the two fighters flashed out of sight into the black of space.

I waited with my fingers just millimeters above the engine control pad. I was not going to miss my cue.

<Chase team, go to burn,> the prince said.

I punched the control pad and it was like we'd been kicked in the back.

SHWWWOOOOOOOOOOOOF!

We were out of there! Out! Of! There!

Unfortunately, we had taken off so fast we'd shot right past the prince's own fighter.

<Ahhhh! Oh, no! No!> I ordered the computer

to match velocity with the other fighters. Something I should have done to start with.

<Hello, Elfangor! Hello-o. You forgot: These old Model Fourteens accelerate faster from a cold start,> Arbron pointed out.

The next thing I heard in my mind was the prince. <You may want to ease back just a little, *Aristh* Elfangor,> he said.

I was relieved he didn't reprimand me. But I was burning with embarrassment. There it was: my big chance to look like a veteran. And I'd looked like an amateur.

I maneuvered my fighter back into formation behind the other two chase fighters.

Arbron brought the Skrit Na raider up on the holographic imager. It was very different than any Andalite ship. Our fighters were elongated ovals with two long, cylindrical engines attached by stubby "wings" on either side. Our main weapon, or shredder, arced overhead much like an Andalite tail.

The Skrit Na ship was round, with tapered sides. It looked like a fat disc. You could hardly even see where the engines were, and the Skrit Na had blinking colored lights all around it. I guess they find that attractive or something.

<Intercept in place,> came the report from the two intercept ships. They had gone into a danger-

ous Maximum Burn to get well out in front of the Skrit Na and cut off escape. Now we just had to sneak up calmly behind them.

Then . . .

<What the. . . . Sir, there is a second Skrit Na ship out here! It was hidden from sensors by the rings of this planet. Repeat, there is a second Skrit Na raider.>

Prince Breeyar rapped his orders. <Okay, you two on intercept go after the *new* target. Everyone else, with me.>

I looked at Arbron. We both nodded. It was getting more complicated now. We could actually have a fight!

Suddenly a bright blue engine flame shot from the bottom of the nearer Skrit Na.

<He's running,> the prince said. He sounded calm, but you could still tell he was excited. There isn't a fighter pilot alive who doesn't enjoy a good chase.

The Skrit Na ship hauled. And we hauled after him.

Then, to my total shock, the Skrit Na fired his weapons!

<Hey, look out!> Arbron yelled.

A thin beam of greenish light lanced toward the prince's fighter. It missed!

<Whoa,> the prince laughed. <That woke me up. Return fire, but only if you can hit the engine pod underneath. Repeat, aim only for the engines. There may be innocent creatures on that ship.>

A split second later, the prince fired and missed. His wingman fired and also missed.

It hadn't even occurred to me that Arbron would actually want to take the risk of shooting. But then he said, <So, Elfangor, how about if we just see how fast this old tub will accelerate?>

I didn't need to be asked twice. I punched up Maximum Burn, and we went to one-tenth light speed in about three seconds!

<Yaaaahhh!> WHAM!

<Yaaaahhh!> WHAM!

The acceleration was outrageous! The compensators were slow and we were thrown back against the bulkhead.

I fought to get back on my feet and to the controls. I renewed my thought-speak link to the computer. <Boost the compensators!>

The computer adjusted and we climbed painfully to our feet. Arbron reached his weapons station and took aim. I heard the hum of the shredder powering up, followed quickly by the sound of firing.

Hmmmm. TSEEEEWWWW!

<Yes! Yes! Yes!> Arbron yelled.

The shredder beam sliced through space and burned away a section of the Skrit Na's engines. The blue engine flame died instantly.

It was the most beautiful thing I'd seen up to that point in my life. But at the same time I felt a wave of jealousy that Arbron had taken the shot and not me.

<Good job,> Prince Breeyar said. <Nice flying, nice shooting.>

Of course he only complimented us because we were *arisths.* I mean, for the regular pilots it would have been no big deal. But who cared? Prince Breeyar had said we did a good job.

<He said "good job,"> Arbron said to me. <He did actually say it, right? I wasn't imagining things?>

<The prince said "good job,"> I confirmed, relishing the words.

At that moment I just loved being alive. I even loved Arbron, as annoying as he was sometimes. This was why I'd joined the military. This was why I'd become an *aristh.* This was what it was all about.

<All right, my little *arisths,*> the prince said affectionately. <Now that you've given us all a lesson in good shooting, show us how you board an enemy ship. Don't forget to download their onboard computer. Is either one of you qualified for exo-datology?>

<*Aristh* Arbron is a very qualified exo-datologist,> I said truthfuly.

Arbron gave me a dirty look.

<Well, you *are*, Arbron,> I said defensively.

See, it's kind of a slight insult to say an *aristh* is good with computers. That's like a technician thing, not a warrior thing. Even though warriors are supposed to be good at all kinds of science and art as well as fighting.

<Good,> the prince said. <And, hey, don't bang your stalks on the low ceilings over there.>

<Yes, sir,> I replied. <No problem.>

I was on top of the universe. I was a hero-in-waiting. Practically a prince already. The war with the Yeerks would be over just as soon as I could get in the game.

I was a fool.

chapter 4

I guess most people know about the Skrit Na. But in case you don't, I'll tell you what I know.

The Skrit Na don't care what anyone else in the galaxy thinks about them. They don't belong to the Yeerk Empire. They aren't one of our allies. They don't care about laws or customs or anything.

All the Skrit Na care about is collecting things and owning things.

The Skrit Na are unusual in another way: They are actually like two different races. The Skrit look like huge insects, almost as large as an Andalite. They have fourteen legs and six sets of antennae, and aren't really very intelligent. But the Skrit each eventually weave a cocoon and a year later, out of the dead Skrit there pops a Na.

The Na are a whole different story. The Na have four very slender legs. Sometimes they rear up and walk on just two legs, using the other legs as hands. They have large heads shaped like Andalite heads, only they have just two huge eyes.

Skrit Na are constantly going to peaceful planets

and kidnapping the local species. Sometimes they perform medical experiments on them. Sometimes they just fly around with them and then let them go. But often they carry local creatures away to add them to zoos on the Skrit Na home world.

Like I said: a weird species. No one understands the Skrit Na. Personally, I don't think they understand themselves.

I pulled our fighter up alongside the damaged Skrit Na ship and turned on the tractor beam to hold the two ships tightly together.

The Skrit Na decided to make it easy. I guess they figured they'd made us mad enough. Skrit Na are no match for Andalite power.

I married my hatch to the Skrit Na hatch and popped it open. I equalized gravities and marched as boldly as I could into the captured ship, with Arbron just behind me.

There was smoke in the other ship. And there seemed to be storage boxes strewn here and there. Two clumsy Skrit lumbered past, kicking through the debris. The ceiling pressed low, and I had to duck my head or risk bruising my stalk eyes. A pair of cocooned Skrit were more or less glued to a corner of the ceiling. One looked about ready to hatch a Na.

There were three Na that I could see. The Na captain was pressed back against his command console. He looked scared. But not of me. He was glaring angrily at a bizarre creature that had a Skrit Na hand weapon, a modified Yeerk Dracon beam, pointed at the Na captain.

The bizarre creature stood just a bit shorter than me. And what was incredible was that it stood on just two legs.

Just two. It had arms, but you could see that it didn't use them to walk. They wouldn't have been long enough.

The creature's face was the same size as mine, but rounder. There were two small bluish eyes on the front of its face. And the lower third of the face was split open horizontally.

Many species have such openings. They're called mouths.

Its body had no fur, but did have brightly colored skin that seemed to hang loosely in some areas. Its upper body was covered in loose, almost billowy, white skin with tiny pastel patterns. Its two legs were covered in a rough-textured blue skin that stopped suddenly at its hooves. The hooves were white and adorned with what looked like thick threads or cables laced together.

But what caught my eye was the hair that sprouted from its head. It was long and wavy and as gold as a yellow sun.

"Freeze, horse-boy," this bizarre creature said,

making the sounds with its mouth. It turned the Dracon beam on me. "One move and I pull the trigger. I don't know what this gun will do, but I'm willing to bet you won't like it."

Of course, at that point all I heard was gibberish sounds. The translator chip, which all members of the Andalite military have implanted in their heads, requires a few minutes to begin to understand new languages. Some languages it never does get right. Fortunately, almost all species can understand our thought-speak since it works at a level beyond mere words.

"Be careful, Andalite friend," the Na captain said. "They are savage, violent beings. Crazy! Wild! Oh, yes! This female is a vicious beast! Better to kill her! Or even better, let us cage her again. Yes, yes, that would be best. As soon as you mistakenly fired on us, she sprang up and grabbed my weapon. Wild and dangerous, oh, yes!"

The translator chip handled the Na language easily. I didn't bother to answer the Na. Everyone knows Skrit Na will lie to anyone about anything.

The Na captain winked one of his big eyes at me. As if he and I were on the same side. His fellow Na officers all looked scared. The Skrit went on with their simple duties like nothing was happening.

To be honest with you, I didn't know what to do. I was as confused as the Skrit Na.

The only one who seemed to have a clue was the bizarre two-legged creature herself.

<Talk to her,> Arbron suggested. <Use your charm, Elfangor.>

<Um . . . whoever you are . . . whatever you are, don't fire that weapon. Put it down.>

"Yeah, right. Hey. Hey, wait a minute! I can hear you in my head, but you're not really talking."

Suddenly the translator chip had heard enough. It began providing instantaneous translation. I could understand her.

<I am in charge here,> I said firmly. <Drop the weapon!>

"Uh-uh. Nope. I don't think so, horse-boy. I'm tired of being kidnapped and dragged off by giant cockroaches and little green men from Mars."

<Excuse me, but we are here to rescue you,> Arbron said.

<Exactly. What these Skrit Na have done to you is wrong. That's why we captured this ship.>

I spoke like I would to a child. Obviously, this species was primitive. They didn't even have tails.

<What little green men?> Arbron asked. <They aren't green. The Na are gray.>

The female narrowed her already narrow eyes. The Dracon beam in her hand wavered. "I'd already captured this ship before you two came along. Me and the other guy. And we're both just kids, which shows you that these Martian jerks aren't all that tough. He's in the back, knocked out. The other guy, I mean. But I grabbed this gun away from Twinkie there." She jerked her head in the direction of the Na captain.

The translator chip had no translation for the word "twinkie." Evidently "twinkie" was some kind of word for "alien."

<Well, we don't mean you any harm,> I said as calmly as I could. <How about this idea? You can keep the Dracon beam, just don't point it at anyone.>

The female looked at the weapon. "It's called a Dracon beam, huh? What's it do?"

Arbron answered before I could suggest he shut up. <It fires an energy beam which causes an exceedingly painful death. Which is why we'd really prefer it if you didn't fire it.>

"Oh. A phaser. Like on that old *Star Trek* show. I can't believe they took that off the air. Now it's just on reruns."

I had nothing to say to that because I had no idea what she was talking about. I looked to Arbron. He shook his head. No, he didn't understand, either. Translator chips have limits.

<If you come with us, we'll treat you well. And we will return you to your home planet.>

"Earth?"

<Is that the name of the third planet in this system?>

"Yeah."

<And are you an Earther?>

"Human. That's what we are: humans. Me and the other guy."

<And we are Andalites. My name is Elfangor. This is Arbron.>

Arbron had gone over to the nearest Skrit Na control panel. He was downloading a copy of all their computer files as Prince Breeyar had ordered. It's standard procedure whenever you board an alien craft.

"You look like centaurs, only with scorpion tails. And the extra eyeballs up on top of your heads . . ." She seemed to hesitate. Suddenly she turned the Dracon beam around and handed it to me, handle first.

<Thank you,> I said. I reached to take the Dracon beam from her and my fingers brushed hers. For some reason I looked at her long golden hair.

"My name is Loren," she said. "This is all kind of amazing. Most humans don't even believe in aliens. But, well, here you are. Real and all. Unless I'm dreaming."

<Do humans dream?> I asked her, surprised.

"I do. Every night."

<So do I. But I guess we have very different dreams.>

Then Loren smiled. It's a thing humans do by turning the corners of their mouths upward. "Maybe," she said. "Maybe not."

chapter 5

We led Loren over to our fighter, and then we carried the second human across. He was unconscious. Bright red blood ran from a cut above his left eye.

<Red blood?> Arbron said. <*Red?* Yuck.>

I was trying to act more mature than Arbron, but to tell you the truth, blood that color creeped me out, too. Still, I didn't think humans looked ugly or anything. Not like the Skrit or Taxxons, which are seriously ugly species. Nor did they look dangerous, like the Hork-Bajir.

Mostly they looked funny. I'd never seen a species that walked on just two legs without even a tail to help with balance. Arbron said what I was thinking. <All it would take is one little push and they'd fall right over. Earth must be hysterical! Humans falling forward and back, falling all over the place. No wonder they are so primitive. They probably spend all their time just trying to stand up.>

We were almost back to the Dome ship when

the second human woke up. We'd left the Skrit Na to try to figure out how to fix their ship. That was their problem.

Hey, no one told them to shoot at us. Right?

"Unh," the human moaned.

He was larger than Loren. Maybe two or three inches larger. His hair was brown, not golden, and it was cut short. His eyes were also brown, not blue like Loren's.

Loren went to him and bent her legs in such a way that she could kneel down beside him. Arbron and I exchanged a look of amazement. It had to be hard to kneel like that and not fall.

"Hey, kid, you okay?" Loren asked.

The wounded human opened his eyes and blinked. He stared hard at me. "What happened?"

Loren shrugged. "Now we have a different bunch of aliens. Who'da guessed there were so many people zipping around outer space? Are you okay? That big cockroach popped you pretty good back there."

<You have nothing to fear,> I said gently. <You are safe now.>

The human felt his wound and looked at the red blood. He seemed almost as grossed out as I was. But he climbed to his feet. Which involved using his hands, I noticed. Humans seem to have stronger hands than we have.

<I am Elfangor. This is Arbron. We are Andalites. We will return you to your home planet.>

The human nodded slowly. "Telepathy. You use telepathy to talk." His gaze traveled to my stalk eyes, back to my face, then to my tail. "That tail is a weapon, isn't it? Is it poisonous or does it just cut?"

I decided right then that I didn't like this human as much as Loren. I didn't like him much at all. <I politely told you my name, human,> I said coldly. <Now, I require *your* name.>

The human gave me a look that seemed insolent. Although who can really tell what an alien facial expression means?

"My name is Hedrick, actually. But I prefer my last name. Most people call me by my last name: Chapman."

"I think these Andalites are okay," Loren said to Chapman. "At least they're better-looking than the last bunch. And they've promised to —"

"Shut up," Chapman snapped. "I'm not interested in the opinion of a kid."

"Kid? Hey, you big jerk, who was it that got the weapon after the ship stopped moving? *Me.* And who was it that was cringing in the back, begging for mercy? *You.* And anyway, I'd be surprised if you're even a year older than me."

Chapman's face grew pink. A fascinating thing

to watch. He clenched his jaw tightly. "And now it seems your heroics were pointless. We're prisoners again. And I have a feeling we won't be grabbing guns away from these Andalites."

Suddenly, he lunged forward toward the Dracon beam in my hand! Without even thinking, I whipped my tail forward and pressed the blade against Chapman's throat.

Chapman laughed. "See that? See how fast he was? Couldn't even see that tail move." Again he gave me an insolent look. "What did you say your species is called? Andalites? Well, I have a feeling you guys are a little more dangerous than you pretend to be, despite all your polite talk and promises."

I felt like a fool. Not for the first time that day. The human Chapman had been testing me.

<We need to prepare to dock with the Dome ship,> Arbron reminded me.

I went through the docking procedure, moving the fighter back inside the fighter bay. I concentrated on my work, but I was upset. I didn't like the human named Chapman. I didn't like his suspicion toward me. After all, we had rescued him from a future as a zoo animal on the Skrit Na home world. He should be grateful.

But maybe that's the way humans are. I've heard

there are species that can't handle anyone helping them. They'd rather die than ever be in debt to someone.

But judging by Loren, not all humans were that way.

Not your problem, Elfangor, I told myself. *Just turn the humans over to the captain. Not your problem at all.*

But I was wrong. The humans *were* my problem.

In fact, I was about to have lots of problems.

chapter 6

<Okay, this part is a little tricky,> I told Loren and Chapman. We were moving from the central shaft out onto the dome floor. There's a ninety-degree gravity change at that point. I mean, "down" in the main shaft is a different direction from "down" on the dome floor. It's confusing at first.

We were safely aboard the *StarSword* and Arbron and I were giving the humans a brief tour. The debriefing officers were too busy to see us yet, I guess, and we couldn't figure out what else to do with the humans.

<You just walk naturally along the curving floor,> I explained. <I know it looks like you're walking off the edge of a cliff, but the artificial gravity will move with you.>

Arbron and I held our breath, watching the ungainly two-legged creatures trying to stay upright. Amazingly, they did it.

<They have very excellent balance,> Arbron whispered.

<They'd have to.>

We emerged from the shaft out onto the grass of the dome and Loren cried out.

"It's huge! It's like a whole park in here! Trees. Grass. Flowers. Wow."

<You have these kinds of things on your planet?> I asked her.

"Well, similar. Our trees are almost always green. And the grass is all green, too. More green than this, I mean, not so much blue. And no red."

<If you are hungry, please feel free to eat as much as you like,> I suggested.

"Eat what?" Chapman asked.

I waved my arm widely to indicate the entire dome. <We have seventeen species of grass in thirty different flavors.>

"Grass? You eat grass?" Loren asked.

Chapman nodded thoughtfully. "That's why you have the dome, isn't it? You graze. Like horses or cows. Only you don't have mouths. So how do you eat?"

<Wait a minute, you eat with your mouths?> Arbron asked.

"How else are you going to eat?" Chapman said.

<With your hooves, like any sensible creature,> Arbron said. Then he laughed. <Do you mean that on Earth humans walk around pressing their mouths to the ground to eat?> He looked at me. <Okay,

even you have to admit *that* would be funny to see.>

Chapman started to explain how humans ate but it was hard to picture, really. It involved spearing chunks of hot, dead animals and stuffing them in the mouth. But I refused to believe that was really how they ate. I assumed Chapman was making things up. Later I found out the truth.

In any case, I was relieved when Loren interrupted Chapman's gruesome story to ask, "Do you mind if I take my shoes off? We've been cooped up in that Skritchy Nose flying saucer. It'd be nice to walk on the grass."

Of course, I had no objection because I had no idea what a "shoe" was. And I could certainly identify with the idea of running on the grass. I was hungry, too.

But then Loren sat down on the grass and began ripping her hooves off! Ripping the very hooves from her legs!

<What are you doing!> I cried. <Stop that! Stop! Why are you hurting yourself?>

"What? What are you yelling about?"

<You're going to hurt yourself, and I don't think our doctors know how to help humans,> I said.

Loren stared at me. She was still holding her leg awkwardly in her two hands. Then she laughed out loud.

It was an alarming, yet strangely pleasing, sound.

"These aren't hooves, Elfangor," she said. "They're shoes. See?" She untied the tiny ropes and before I could stop her, she ripped the white hoof clear off!

<Noooo!> I moaned.

<Ahhhh!> Arbron yelled.

But Loren was not in pain. And there was no blood. Then she removed a layer of white skin from the exposed leg end. Suddenly, I was staring at five tiny pink fingers. They were growing from her leg.

"See? This is my foot. We don't have hooves. And we wear shoes over our feet. See? They keep the rocks or whatever from hurting our feet."

I felt a wave of intense pity. What had gone wrong in the evolution of this species? The entire species had to cover its "feet" to keep from being injured? An entire race crippled?

Suddenly the funny mental image of a planet of humans falling over all the time was replaced by the sad picture of a species of cripples, hobbling along on their weak, injured "feet" and covering them with artificial hooves.

Loren stood up on her delicate pink feet with their ridiculous, short pink fingers and started to run across the grass. She wasn't very fast, but she obviously wasn't crippled.

And then she did something amazing. She

turned her head around. She turned the entire thing so it was pointing backward. "Come on!"

But I couldn't move. I noticed Arbron was as amazed as I was.

<What the . . . what's she doing?> he asked. Then it dawned on him. <It's because they only have two eyes! They turn their heads around to see behind them!>

I stifled an urge to laugh. I broke into a gentle trot and quickly caught up to Loren.

"Feels . . . good . . . to stretch . . . my muscles," she said, speaking in a halting way as she ran.

She stopped running and twirled around. Twirled right around, and her golden hair flew out behind her. That was something to see. A two-legged creature can twirl better than a normal person.

"I was sure I was going to die on that flying saucer," she said. "But here I am! Amazing."

<I guess this all seems very strange.>

"Oh, yeah. Strange isn't half of it. This is a beautiful tree. Pink leaves. Incredible."

<It's called a *therant* tree. It's in its *creast* phase. Do you see the way the grasses become more *gelasic* and less *escalic* as they grow near? That is because —>

I stopped talking then, because Loren casually reached up and touched a low branch. There was nothing wrong with that, of course. But then she wrapped both her hands around the branch and lifted herself clear up off the ground!

That alone was a miracle. But as she stretched, I saw the white, pastel-marked skin of her upper body come loose! It lifted away and revealed a layer of pinkish, tan underneath that matched her face and arm skin.

Arbron came running, with Chapman struggling to catch up.

Loren held herself suspended and laughed at us. I guess we'd been staring.

<Very strong arms!> Arbron remarked. <Can you imagine lifting your whole body up with your arms?>

<That skin is very strange,> I said. <It's almost as if it's not attached.>

Loren let herself drop back to the grass. And she didn't even fall over.

"It's not skin," Chapman said. "It's called clothing. Like the artificial hooves? This is artificial skin. It keeps us warm."

<You're cold?>

"No. But that's why we have clothing. To keep us warm in cold places."

<Why would you be in cold places?> I asked, curiosity overcoming my dislike for the human.

He shrugged his powerful human shoulders. Shoulders capable of lifting his entire body. "Parts of

Earth are very cold. Parts of it are so cold you'd die without many layers of clothing."

<But why do you live in those places?> I asked.

Chapman smiled. It was interesting, because already I was getting the feeling that not all human smiles were pleasant. "We're not going to be kept out of a place just because the weather's bad. We adapt. We grab whatever's available and make the best of it. At least that's my motto: Grab what you can."

I would have asked him more, but just then the call came for Arbron to go to debriefing. And I was ordered to take the humans to a holding room.

chapter 7

<What? WHAT? Leave the ship?!> I screeched.
<What do you mean, leave the ship?!>

Arbron did not look any happier than I was.
<They just *told* me, okay? They didn't ask my opin-
ion. The captain called me from debriefing, had me
run to the bridge, said, "You and *Aristh* Elfangor be
at Docking Bay Seven in ten minutes," and I said,
"Yes, sir.">

I had taken the humans to a holding room. And
then, while waiting for my own debriefing I'd gone
back to the dome to eat. I was very hungry. I was on
my way to check back on Loren when Arbron inter-
cepted me.

<This can't be right,> I moaned. <The *StarSword*
is my home. We're going to find that Yeerk task
force and destroy them.>

<Yeah, yeah, I know. And you'll be a big hero
and they'll make you a prince without even slowing
down to make you a warrior.>

<That's not what I was thinking,> I lied.

<Well, forget it. Come on. We move out immediately. We're supposed to meet up with our commander for this mission.>

Something about the tone of Arbron's thought-speak made me wary. <Our commander? Who's our commander?>

<None other than War-prince Alloran-Semitur-Corrass,> Arbron said.

Both my hearts sank into my hooves. Alloran. Alloran, the disgraced. So this mission was definitely not a reward from the captain. Alloran had once been a great warrior and prince. But he had been disgraced. I didn't know why. No one talked about it. Everyone just knew that Alloran had broken some law or custom.

Being sent off on some stupid side mission with a disgraced war-prince was not a good thing.

I couldn't believe it. This ship was my home. I didn't want to leave her, not even for a while. It could take a long time before we could rejoin the *StarSword,* and by then, who knew? Maybe by some miracle the entire war would be over.

Which would be good, I supposed.

<What's in Docking Bay Seven, anyway?> I grumbled as we reached the right door.

Arbron swung his stalks back and forth in a "who knows?" gesture.

We opened the door to Docking Bay Seven. And there, standing awkwardly on their two legs, were Loren and Chapman. Behind them stood Alloran.

I had seen War-prince Alloran around the Dome ship at times. He'd always seemed to be deep in thought. Like he was off somewhere in his imagination or memory. He was not especially large. But he seemed to be carved from solid steel. Even his fur was a metallic blue. And the bare flesh of his upper body showed faint traces of burn scars.

Beyond Alloran was a ship I had never seen before. It hovered just inches above the polished floor. It was three times the size of any fighter I'd ever encountered. The main section was a fantastically elongated oval that stretched way out in front of three oversized, swept-back engines. Three engines, not the usual two! And coming up overhead was the long, gracefully arced spike of the main shredder.

Oh, she was a thing of beauty. I had never fallen in love with a machine before, but, oh, that ship was sweet.

<I see you like my little toy, *aristh*,> Alloran said.

<It's the most beautiful thing I've ever seen,> I said. <Like . . . like a work of art.>

<I designed her myself. I call her the *Jahar*. It's my wife's name.>

<Prince Alloran, what is our mission?> Arbron asked.

The prince sighed a little, but when he spoke he was firm and correct. <We are to take these two aliens back to their planet, erase their recent memories, and rejoin the *StarSword* whenever we can.>

<Transport work,> I said. I didn't exactly sneer, but I felt like sneering. We were just running a silly errand.

"Excuse me? Erase my memory?" Loren said. "No one is erasing my memory."

<It's necessary,> I said as kindly as I could. <Your civilization is not ready for what you've encountered. If you go back to your Earth, you'll have to have all memory of this erased.>

The two humans looked at each other. The one called Chapman made a snorting sound from his nose. Loren made a facial expression that looked troubled. At least that's how it looked to me.

<Let's move, *arisths*,> Alloran ordered. <Load the aliens. The captain wants to go to Z-space five minutes from now, and by then we have to be well clear of the Dome ship. Your personal belongings have already been brought from your quarters.>

No one was in a good mood as we walked up the ramp into the *Jahar*. The humans were stone-faced, angry, perhaps afraid. Arbron and I were both grim, feeling we'd been shoved off on some stupid side trip. And Alloran could not have been exactly thrilled, either. He was a great war-prince. And here he was running errands with only a pair of *arisths* under his command.

The one good thing was the *Jahar*. It was as beautiful inside as out. There were small but luxurious quarters. And there was good green and blue grass under our feet, not hard steel. By some trick of gravity manipulation Alloran had even created a small waterfall in one corner that went down, splashed into a pool, then fell back upward to fall all over again.

Alloran took the helm, which left Arbron and me with nothing to do. He executed a smooth launch out of the docking bay, and then, suddenly, we were out in black space, looking up through the real windows at the Dome ship.

The *StarSword* was silhouetted against the bright rings of the sixth planet.

"Oh, my God," Loren gasped. "That's Saturn!"

As I watched, the *StarSword*'s engines glowed brilliant blue and the Dome ship picked up speed. Faster and faster, till suddenly, with a flash, she translated into Zero-space and disappeared.

"Faster-than-light travel?" Chapman marveled. "It's physically impossible!"

<True. But Z-space travel doesn't involve going

fast. It involves tunneling through anti-space, what we call Zero-space, and then back into the normal universe at another point,> Arbron said.

"But I suppose you Andalites keep the secret to yourselves, eh?" Chapman said.

<Not always,> Alloran said darkly. <Once we shared it. The result was the Yeerk Empire that threatens all decent species. Be glad you are safe on your simple planet, alien. The galaxy is not a happy place to be anymore.>

Alloran entered the destination into the computer. We would make one brief Zero-space jump to approach Earth. But Z-drive travel is not very precise. Even if we were lucky, we'd probably emerge a million miles from Earth itself. It would be a trip of many days to get there.

<Make the aliens comfortable, *arisths,*> Alloran ordered.

<Prince, afterward may I use your ship's computers?> Arbron asked. <I have a copy of the Skrit Na download and I thought I spotted something strange.>

<An exo-datologist, eh?> Alloran said with a slight sneer. <The new ideal: warrior, scientist, artist. It's not enough to be a fighter anymore, eh? They want a gentler, more balanced, more intellectual sort of warrior nowadays.>

Arbron looked helplessly at me. <I guess so,

War-prince Alloran. I mean, that's what they teach us, anyway.>

For a while Alloran said nothing. He just stared blankly, not at anyone. Or at least not at anyone in that room. <The Electorate wants war without slaughter. They want a clean, neat, honorable war. Fools.>

I was shocked. You didn't call the Electorate fools. You just didn't.

<Sir . . . ,> Arbron asked timidly. <The computer . . . ?>

<What? Oh, yes. The computer. Why not? Use it all you like,> the prince said. <We're in for a long, boring ride.>

chapter 8

It <u>was</u> a long, boring trip. We came out of Zero-space halfway between the orbits of Earth and a planet Loren called Mars.

We had to travel through conventional space. And we had to keep our speed down so as not to distort time too much. If we'd gone to Maximum Burn all the way to Earth, we'd have gotten there in a few hours. But on the planet, years would have passed. That's relativity for you.

I had little to do. Alloran brooded alone at the helm, or else went to his quarters. And Arbron seemed to have found some project to keep him busy. He spent his time at the computer, muttering.

It was a side of Arbron I'd never really seen. Mostly he never seemed to take anything very seriously. At least he never took *me* seriously. But now he was spending days at the console.

Whenever I asked him what he was doing, he'd just say, <Unraveling a mystery.>

So I spent most of my time with the two humans. Or at least with Loren. Chapman was as

51

brooding as Alloran. I stood beside Loren at the window, and looked out at the blue and white planet.

Loren did a thing she called "sitting." It's funny to see at first. But of course very practical for a two-legged creature.

"The brown-and-green parts are land," Loren was explaining. "The blue is ocean. Water. See the bright white at the bottom? That's ice. It's called Antarctica. It's very cold."

<What sort of ice? Frozen carbon dioxide? Methane?>

"Water. Just frozen water."

<Ah. Of course. That would make sense. And where do you live?>

"Well, see that continent there? The one on the upper left part of the planet? See where the line between night and day is? Almost right on that line." She bit her lip. A lip is a mouth part. "My mom must be dying from worry. I've been gone for four days already."

Dying? Humans could die of emotion? <Yes, but soon you will be home. Then she won't worry anymore. Maybe she won't have to die.>

Loren smiled. "That's just an expression."

Then I noticed that there were glistening drops in her eyes.

"Do you have a mother at home? Does she worry about you?"

I felt a little uncomfortable talking about my parents. An *aristh* in deep space can't start getting all homesick. Especially since Prince Alloran was nearby, able to overhear everything.

<I guess she does. My father doesn't, though. He was in the military, too, when he was young. Of course, we had peace then. I guess maybe they do worry I'll get hurt or whatever.>

"We just had a war," Loren said. "That's . . . that's what happened to my dad. He was in it. He didn't get killed or anything. But he kind of . . . I don't know. After he came back I guess he couldn't cope with reality. So he left."

I saw Alloran's stalk eyes swivel to look at Loren. It was practically the first time he'd even noticed her.

<You have wars?> I asked. <But you don't have space travel. Who do you fight?>

Chapman arrived then, having arisen from a nap in his quarters. "We fight each other," he said. He winked one eye. "So, Loren, Daddy went nutso, huh? Another whacked-out 'Nam vet? I guess some guys can't take it."

Loren's eyes went wide, and then she turned on Chapman.

But it was Alloran who spoke. <Have you been in a war, human?> he asked Chapman.

"Me? No. Of course not. That war's over."

<Then be quiet, fool. Those who have been to war understand. Those who have not have no opinion worth hearing.> He looked directly at Loren. <Even those who return from war may never really come home.>

Alloran turned his stalk eyes back to the helm, and said nothing more. Chapman shrugged, but I could see he was intrigued by Alloran.

So was I, to be honest. What was he talking about? I'd never heard of an Andalite warrior coming back from the war unable to cope, as Loren had put it. Or "whacked-out," as Chapman had said. Why would Alloran feel such sympathy?

"Anyway . . . ," Loren began, "tell me this. When you erase my memory, I won't remember any of this? Not even you?"

I didn't answer. What could I say?

"It's okay, I'm not mad at you," Loren said. "You're taking us home. And you saved us from those Skritchy Noses."

<Skrit Na,> I corrected.

"I know. It was a joke. Maybe not a very funny joke, I guess."

<Ah. Humor. Yes, Arbron does that sometimes.>

"But not you?"

<I guess I'm not very funny.>

Loren tossed her head in such a way that her long golden hair shimmered very nicely. "That's okay. I like serious guys. I guess if my memory is going to be erased, it won't hurt if I ask questions. So. How come you don't have mouths?" she asked.

Chapman seemed to snap out of a reverie. He'd been looking at Alloran. Now he joined the conversation. "Loren, how can he answer that question? He doesn't have a mouth. We do. Why do we have mouths? Stupid question. I have a better question." He looked closely at me, focusing first on my stalk eyes, and then back down on my main eyes. Like he couldn't make up his mind where to look.

"Look, Elfangor, maybe we got off to a bad start, you and me. I wasn't in a great mood, you know? But hey, you guys are really missing out on something here. Do you have any idea how much money we could get for this technology on Earth? I mean, you could ask for anything!"

It was my turn to laugh. <What would we do with Earth money?>

He shrugged. "Okay, forget money. How about power? We could snap our fingers and have all the presidents and prime ministers on Earth waiting on us. We could rule."

<We're Andalites,> I said, <not Yeerks. We aren't interested in ruling other species.>

"Ah. Well, that's good, I guess. Yeah, that's a good thing. But we could bring peace to Earth. No more wars."

<Okay. That's it. That's it. Elfangor!> It was Arbron. He'd been totally absorbed in staring at the computer display. He'd barely spoken for the last two days.

I went to him. I was glad to be away from Chapman. He bothered me. He was completely different than the human Loren.

<What is it?> I asked Arbron as I came to stand beside him. I looked past him to the computer display. It showed a power field, lines of intensity in three dimensions. But it also showed lines extending strongly into Zero-space.

It was impossible. A simulation of some sort. A fake.

Arbron turned only his stalk eyes toward me. <This is from the Skrit Na ship. From the computer download. It was encrypted, but I broke the code. I've been going through the ship's log. A bunch of stupid stuff, mostly. Junk. But yesterday I found this. I've been trying to figure it out, because, see, there's no way these sensor readings can be right. But now I think I've got it. I know what it is.> He turned all the way to face me. <Elfangor, I think this is *real*.>

For several seconds we both just stared at each

other. <This can't be,> I said. <Any first-year student could tell you this is impossible. Unless . . .> I felt a chill run up my spine. <Alloran! Prince Alloran! Sir, you should see this.>

The prince turned away from the helm and trotted back to us. <What is it, *arisths?*> he said wearily. But then his stalk eyes focused on the screen. A second later he was staring with full intensity at the image there. <Computer. Cross-check for any visual files!> To Arbron and me he said, <They would have made more recordings!>

And then it appeared. It simply appeared on the computer screen.

It was perfectly spherical. A simple white sphere.

It looked harmless, even dull. And yet it was the most dangerous, deadly weapon any race had ever created.

Because of what it was, it could not be physically destroyed. But it had been hidden. As we watched, dumbfounded and afraid, the computer replayed the Skrit Na computer log.

It had been hidden on the planet called Earth. It had been buried deep in the ground in a desolate-looking area of blowing sand. And a huge stone pyramid had been raised over it.

Hidden for fifty thousand years.

Hidden on an insignificant planet at the far end of the galaxy. And now it had reappeared.

"Hey, what's the matter with you guys?" Loren asked. "You all look like you've seen a ghost."

<The Time Matrix!> Arbron said. <I thought it was just a myth.>

<The second Skrit Na ship!> I yelled, suddenly realizing the truth. <The Skrit Na dug it up. They have it aboard the second ship, the one that escaped into Zero-space!>

I looked to Alloran. To my surprise, his eyes were alight with fierce pleasure. <The Time Matrix! Hidden for fifty thousand years, and now dug up by the Skrit Na. The deadliest weapon in all of galactic history . . . and no one but us to go and get it back.>

It was as if Alloran were suddenly ten years younger. <Elfangor! Arbron! Get back on that Skrit Na computer log, both of you. We need to know where that second ship ran to! *Now!*>

He turned to Loren and Chapman. <I apologize, aliens, but we cannot take you straight back to your planet. There is no time to waste. The existence of the entire galaxy is at stake!>

Arbron looked at me and sent me a private thought-speak message. <I guess we may still get a chance at being heroes.>

chapter 9

Arbron and I tore that Skrit Na computer download apart. And before we translated into Zerospace we had a destination in mind. One of the last places in the universe that any sensible Andalite would ever want to go.

The Taxxon home world.

As we spent timeless time traveling through the blank white nondistance of Zero-space, Alloran called a council. It was just for the three of us, but the *Jahar* was too small for us to keep the two humans out. They squatted on the floor near our hooves.

We excluded them from our thought-speak at first, keeping our conversation private.

<Taxxon home world is our destination,> Alloran said. <But the Skrit Na would *not* be taking the Time Matrix there. So I believe the Skrit Na don't know what they have. They saw strange power patterns and decided, with the usual Skrit Na simplemindedness, to steal first and figure it out later.>

<I agree, sir,> Arbron said. <If they knew they

had the Time Matrix they'd do one of two things. Head straight for the Yeerk home world to sell it to the Yeerks. Or else head home to use it for their own people. But the Taxxon home world is —>

"Hey. Hey!" Chapman interrupted. "You're doing your little telepathy thing and keeping us out. I'm not an idiot."

<This does not involve either of you,> I said curtly.

Chapman stood up and grabbed me roughly by the shoulder. I twitched my tail out of reflex. No Andalite would ever grab another Andalite.

Chapman laughed rudely. "You don't scare me. I know you can kill us both. But that's not your style, is it? Dragging us off across the galaxy *is* your style."

<We have an emergency,> I said. <We regret that we cannot take you straight back to your planet. However —>

"However nothing," Chapman said. "This little trip involves danger, doesn't it? You boys are in deep. Like I said, I'm not an idiot. I can see you three are tense. I can see you're worried. Wherever it is we're going, you're scared. Which means me and the girl here should be afraid, too, right?"

Loren stood up and looked right at me. "Is that true, Elfangor? Are you taking us into danger?"

I turned one eye toward Alloran. He nodded slightly, giving me permission.

<Yes, Loren,> I said. <We are going into terrible danger. If we are taken, the two of you will be killed or enslaved.>

Chapman's eyes blazed. "You're dragging us into a battle and we can't even know what's going on? Is that Andalite fairness?"

I started to tell the annoying creature to be silent, but Alloran spoke.

<You two aliens have a right to know what you are being "dragged into," as you put it. We are going to a planet of creatures who are allies of the Yeerks. The Yeerks are parasites who seize control of the bodies and minds of other creatures. The Taxxons have been enslaved this way. By their own choice.>

I said, <The Skrit Na have apparently discovered the long-lost Time Matrix. This is a device that allows people to move forward or backward in time. It is the most dangerous weapon imaginable.>

"Why would a time machine be a weapon?" Loren asked.

But Chapman had already figured it out. "Duh. I go back in time and change history to wipe you out in the present. I could kill your parents before they had you, and you'd never exist." He grinned. "Better yet, I could go all the way back in time, back to prehistoric days and find the earliest ancestors of humans and kill them. The entire human race would cease to exist." Chapman laughed. "I see why you guys are worried. If these Yeerks of yours get this thing, it's bye-bye Andalites."

That did it. I didn't like this creature. I didn't care if he was just a primitive alien, I didn't like him. I pushed my face close to his. I brought my tail up into a threat position. <You'd better understand something, human. If it's "bye-bye" Andalites, it'll be "bye-bye" humans, sooner or later. Who do you think keeps the Yeerks from conquering every sentient race in the galaxy? *We* do.>

"Maybe I'm with the wrong aliens," Chapman sneered. "Maybe it's too bad I wasn't grabbed by the Yeerks. They sound like the winners."

To my surprise, Prince Alloran actually laughed. <You may be right, human. But you'd better hope you're not. I've seen what the Yeerks do to captive planets. I was there when the Yeerks took the Hork-Bajir world. Pray to whatever primitive gods you have, human, that the Yeerks don't *ever* take your world.>

I shot a glance at Arbron. He was as surprised as I was. Alloran had been there at the loss of the Hork-Bajir world?

The loss of the Hork-Bajir was the single biggest disaster in our war with the Yeerks. The Hork-Bajir were the slave warriors of the Yeerk Empire now because we'd failed to save them.

<Translation to normal space in one minute,> the computer announced without emotion.

<Okay,> Alloran said, breaking the spell he had cast over us all. <We'll be coming out of Z-space fairly close to the Taxxon world. The area will be thick with Yeerk ships. The *Jahar* has excellent stealth shielding, but we may still be detected. From now on, we are on battle alert.>

<What's the plan?> Arbron asked nervously. <What do we do?>

Alloran laughed. <What's the plan? We locate the Skrit Na ship. And if it has landed, we go down after it and take back the Time Matrix. Of course, we'd be a little obvious walking around as Andalites. So . . .>

<Down to the surface of the Taxxon world?> I asked in horror. <You mean . . . sir, are you planning for us to morph Taxxons?>

Alloran looked very seriously at Arbron and me. <You two *arisths* are going to have to grow up very fast now. I need warriors at my side. Are you ready to be warriors?>

In my daydreams as a young *aristh* I had imagined a moment like this. I had imagined a time coming when I would be called upon to be brave and to save my people. And in my imagination I had always faced this kind of moment with pride and without fear.

And now, suddenly, my daydream was reality. And all I felt was sick dread.

The Taxxon world! It was a place from a nightmare.

<We're ready, Prince Alloran,> I said, as boldly as I could. <We are ready to be your warriors. We're not afraid.>

I saw Arbron's face. He was as sick with fear as I was. But still he managed to smirk. He knew me too well.

He knew I was lying.

chapter 10

Down to the Taxxon world!

The *Jahar* was cloaked, hidden from sight and from most sensors. But a close sensor sweep by a Yeerk ship would reveal us. And we would never be able to land on the planet in the *Jahar*.

We needed a victim.

We found it, out beyond the Taxxon world's third moon. It was a slow-moving transport ship. It was just arriving in the system, which meant they would be expecting it down on the surface. Perfect for our needs.

The trick was to disable the ship — to make it stop, but not destroy it.

<This will take precise aim,> Alloran said. <Which of you two is a better shot?>

I wanted to say that I was. But I knew Arbron was better. And we could not afford to fail. <Arbron is the one who hit the Skrit Na ship.>

Alloran nodded. <Let's see what you can do, *Aristh* Arbron. We need to hit one engine, but leave

the other functioning. And we don't want any un-fortunate explosions.>

Arbron took the shredder controls in his hands. The Yeerk transport ship was two thousand miles away. The target engine was about forty feet long.

Arbron keyed into the computer targeting sys-tem and made careful adjustments while all of us — Alloran, the two humans, and I — watched.

There was a hum as the shredder fired. We saw the pale green beam lance forward into darkness. And on the screen, with magnification at factor five hundred, we saw the near-side engine pod of the Yeerk ship glow red and green.

<Good shooting!> Alloran said. <They'll waste half an hour trying to figure out what happened and reconfiguring to fly with just one engine. *Aristh* Elfangor, take us in fast!>

I punched up a burn and we rocketed forward, descending on the crippled transport. We were alongside the transport before they knew we were there.

<Jam their communications,> Alloran ordered, and I feverishly punched the flat surface of the tacti-cal board with my fingers.

It was my second boarding of an alien vessel. I guess I should have felt like I was an old hand. But this wasn't some lame bunch of Skrit Na. This was a Yeerk ship. We had no way of knowing what we would encounter. Would it be Hork-Bajir-Con-trollers? Taxxon-Controllers? Or some other fierce, unknown species the Yeerks controlled?

<A word of advice,> Alloran said. <Taxxons may be repulsive, but never forget that down in their brains they have a Yeerk. You're dealing with a Yeerk, not just a Taxxon.>

Alloran, Arbron, and I pressed close to the hatch, waiting for it to blow open. We carried handheld shredders on setting three. There are six power levels on a shredder. Level one delivers a mild charge that will stun a small creature for a moment or two. Level six will blast a hole through ten feet of solid alloy. Level three wouldn't kill most creatures, but it would certainly knock them down so hard they wouldn't get up for hours.

At that moment, waiting to rush a deadly enemy, I struggled to recall everything old Sofor had ever tried to teach me about combat. But I swear I couldn't remember a word. Maybe Prince Alloran was calm, but I sure wasn't.

<Remember, don't kill them all,> Alloran said. <We may need to acquire them.>

"Good luck," Loren said.

And then the hatch blew.

BOOM!

In a rush of wind from the explosion, we launched ourselves into the Yeerk transport. Taxxons!

If you've never faced a Taxxon, let me tell you: They are shocking things to see up close. They are tubular, like a monstrously thick, ten-foot-long hose. They have rows of needle-sharp, cone-shaped legs. The upper third of their body is held upright, and there the rows of legs become smaller and form tiny two- and three-fingered hands.

There is a row of dark red eyes, each like congealed liquid. At the very top is the mouth, a round, red-rimmed hole circled with vicious rows of teeth.

There were half a dozen of these creatures practically encircling us. For a frozen moment no one moved. I don't think the Yeerks could quite believe that they were being boarded by Andalites, right there in orbit around the Taxxon home world.

Then everyone unfroze at once!

On my left, one Taxxon raised a Dracon beam and aimed it at me.

<Ahhh!> I yelled and pulled the trigger of my shredder.

TTTTSSSAAAPPP!

The Taxxon crumpled.

TTTTSSSSAAAAPPP! TTTTSSSSAAAPPPP!

Shredders fired.

TSEEEEWWW! TSEEEEWWW! TSEEEWWW!

Dracon beams fired!

The air was instantly as hot as an oven. Shock waves from all the weapons rocked the enclosed

68

area. Screens blew out. Sheet-plastic panels crumpled. Sparks exploded in brilliant waterfalls from popped conduits overhead.

<Stop firing!> Alloran ordered. <We'll destroy the ship!>

Behind me, a Taxxon! Dracon beam coming up!

I didn't pause to think. I just jerked my tail. My tail blade sliced through the air and separated the Taxxon's arm from his body. The arm fell to the deck, still weakly clutching the Dracon beam.

"SSSRRREEEE-WWWAAARR!" the Taxxon screamed.

Now there were only two Taxxons still standing, and they knew they were beaten. They backed away as fast as they could motor their cone legs. But even then, and even with the Yeerks in their heads, the Taxxons' evil instincts would not be denied. As they backed away they bent low to tear chunks of flesh from their dead companions.

The Taxxons are cannibalistic. Not a nice species. And according to everything we knew about them, not even the Yeerks inside them could control that foul hunger of theirs.

<All right!> Arbron cried. <We got 'em!>

<Shut up, you young fool,> Alloran snapped.

Alloran had already guessed why the Taxxon-Controllers were pulling back. They didn't want to be in the way when serious trouble showed up.

And that serious trouble was just becoming visible through the haze of smoke from burning, sparking panels.

Seven feet tall. Razor-sharp blades at the wrists. Razor-sharp blades at their elbows. And knees. And tails. And two or three huge, forward-swept horn-blades on the tops of their snakelike heads.

Hork-Bajir!

<Well, well,> Alloran said, <it's been a while since I fought a Hork-Bajir. I'll take the two big ones in the middle.>

That left a Hork-Bajir warrior each for me and Arbron.

Two full-grown, adult Hork-Bajir, each with a wily Yeerk in its head.

<I'm thinking maybe we should both have paid more attention to old Sofor,> Arbron said, making a grim joke.

I saw the Hork-Bajir advance on me. I heard Sofor's voice in my head. *Don't think, Elfangor. It's all instinct and training now.*

I let go of my conscious mind. I simply let it slip away. And in its place, a tingling energy seemed to fill me up. It was as if I were charged with electricity. As if sparks might fly from my hooves and tail.

The Hork-Bajir came on toward me. And I struck.

I struck!

And when Alloran was outflanked by one of his opponents, I struck again.

And when Arbron was knocked down by his Hork-Bajir opponent, I struck again.

I struck and struck and struck till Hork-Bajir blood ran on the decks.

And when my own conscious mind returned, it seemed as if hours had gone by. Arbron was staring at me like he'd seen a ghost. Alloran was nodding grimly, as if he recognized something about me.

Wounded Hork-Bajir, and worse than wounded, were lying in Taxxon gore on the deck.

<No,> I whispered.

I turned and ran back through the hatch to the *Jahar*.

I ran and slipped and fell to my knees, with nowhere else to run.

It was the human, Loren, who ran to me and put her strange human arms around my chest and with one hand pressed my face into her long golden hair.

chapter 11

I shook myself free of Loren, appalled and ashamed by my behavior. What was the matter with me? I was behaving like a child, not an *aristh*.

Then I saw Arbron.

He had been cut. He was bleeding from a deep gash in his left arm. His main eyes were wide with what might almost have been panic.

Alloran was busy tying up the injured Hork-Bajir. The injured Taxxons were shoved into a small storeroom. Alloran sealed them in by welding the door with his shredder.

"Are you okay?" Loren asked me.

<Yes. Of course. I'm fine,> I said harshly. But my insides were churning. Some awful feeling was eating into my thoughts. I felt stunned. I felt like I wasn't even me. It was like I was some totally different person, standing off to one side, just watching myself.

Loren left me alone and went to Arbron. She tore the sleeve off her shirt and wrapped it around Arbron's bleeding arm.

Alloran came over and glanced at Arbron's arm. <You'll be okay, *aristh,*> he said. <Go back to the weapons station. We've just started here. We have to fly this Yeerk crate down to the planet. *Aristh* Elfangor, you take the helm. The controls are more primitive than our own ships, but —>

Neither Arbron nor I had moved. Alloran glared at me, furious that I was ignoring his order. But then I saw his expression soften.

<It's your first time. You fought well. Both of you. It's always hard the first time. And it never gets easy. But I need you both. Now.>

I nodded. <Yes, Prince Alloran. I'll take the helm.>

<You. Alien,> he said to Loren. <Get back into the *Jahar.* We'll be away for a while. Don't touch anything.>

Loren turned her head to look back over her shoulder. Humans have to do that in order to see behind them. She was obviously hesitating. She bit her lower lip with her short white teeth.

<What is it?> I asked.

Still she hesitated. Then, "Look, tell me the truth. Swear by whatever it is that is really important to you. Swear that you're going to take Chapman and me back to Earth."

<Of course we are. As soon as we can,> I said.

She sighed, a sound that involved blowing air out of her mouth. "Look, it's Chapman. I'm sure he's a nice guy and all, really . . ."

<You don't trust him.>

"If you leave the two of us here on the *Jahar*, he'll try something. I know he will. And I know you think we're too primitive to be able to fly your ship or whatever, but don't count on it. Chapman doesn't like you."

<Yes. I got that impression,> I said. <But we can tell the ship's computer not to allow him to do anything. He won't be able to fly the ship or use communications. It will be all right.> With my stalk eyes I saw that Prince Alloran was busy with Arbron. <Here. Take this. Hide it under your clothing. Use it if Chapman makes trouble for you. It is set to level two. Just point it and squeeze the trigger.>

Loren took the shredder from me and slipped it under her shirt. "Listen . . . good luck down on the planet. Whatever you're doing down there."

Then she put her face close to mine and pressed her lips against the side of my face. It was a very odd thing to do. Not something any Andalite would ever do. And yet I did not mind it.

<*Aristh* Elfangor? Whenever you have the time to join us . . . ,> Alloran said acidly.

<Ready, sir! Preparing to sever the connection with the *Jahar*.>

The hatch closed, shutting Loren the human off from sight.

She would be all right, I told myself. The *Jahar* was well-shielded. With the engines off it would be almost impossible for the Yeerks to detect. And she had the shredder in case the other human tried to start trouble.

I focused on understanding the ship's controls. They were designed for Taxxon hands. But the basics were still the basics. I calculated a simple approach to the Taxxon world's main spaceport. I fired the engines and then, as we moved away, gathering speed, I looked back and saw the *Jahar*.

<These humans are a pain in the hindquarters,> Arbron said. <As if we don't have enough trouble? We have to watch over a pair of primitive aliens?>

<She's a million light-years from her home, Arbron. Confronting species she never knew existed. Suddenly thrust into the middle of an intergalactic war. I think she is very brave.>

Arbron busied himself with learning the computer station of the strange ship. But then, in a carefully offhand way, he said, <By the way, thanks. You saved my life back there. I guess you absorbed more from old Sofor than you thought, huh?>

<I guess so,> I said.

<You were something, Elfangor. You scared me. Hey, I think you even scared Alloran. You really —>

<Okay, shut up, all right?>

<I was just saying you were great back there. Faster-than-light tail action. When you cut that one big Hork-Bajir's head? That was amazing.>

I wanted Arbron to shut up. I didn't want to think about what had happened. I didn't want to remember it.

And yet this other part of me was hanging on every word. This other part of me was replaying the fight in my head, seeing myself as Elfangor, the great hero.

<Course laid in?> Alloran asked me.

<Yes, Prince. We should be arriving in thirty minutes.>

<Good. Then it's time. We need to acquire the Taxxons.>

To acquire is to absorb the DNA of a species. It is the first step in morphing that creature.

We were going to become Taxxons.

chapter 12

We had shoved the Taxxons and the badly wounded Hork-Bajir into the cargo hold of the ship. We had not even looked into the hold to see what else might be in there.

Now we looked.

We opened the door and Alloran and Arbron stood with their shredders ready in case the surviving Taxxons tried to attack us. But the two Taxxons had other things on their minds.

They were attempting to kill and eat each other. They had already finished off the wounded Hork-Bajir.

<Stop it or I'll kill you both!> Alloran yelled.

But the Taxxons were out of control, caught up in their own evil bloodlust. It was a vile thing to watch. Taxxons don't have powerful tails like us, or blades like the Hork-Bajir. They can only rear up and slam their upper bodies against each other while trying to gouge with their round mouths.

<Their Yeerks have left them,> Alloran said. <This is how Taxxons behave when they are not

Controllers. Their Yeerk parasites have left them to destroy each other.>

<Where did the Yeerks go?> I asked.

Alloran calmly leveled his shredder at the Taxxons and fired. It was a low-level blast, just enough to knock the Taxxons unconscious.

We stepped past their sagging bodies, careful to keep our hooves out of the gore. Behind them, the hold of the ship was filled with transparent circular tanks. It was too dark to see what was in the tanks.

<Computer. Lights,> Alloran said.

Lights came on, and I instantly wished they hadn't.

The hold of the ship stretched for perhaps a hundred feet straight back, with a width of a third that. Filling most of that space, glowing a sludgy green, were dozens of tanks.

And in each tank, swimming through the viscous liquid, were gray slugs.

<Yeerks!> I said.

<There must be thousands! Tens of thousands!> Arbron said.

<I suspected this might be the case,> Alloran said. <These are Yeerks being transported to the Taxxon world. They're here to get bodies. Hosts. Each of these will be given a Taxxon.>

<What do we do with them?> I asked.

<We seal the bridge then open the outer hatch,> Alloran said calmly.

It took me a few seconds to realize what he was saying. If we opened the outer hatch while we were still in space, the vacuum would suck everything in the hold out. Out into the airless cold. The Yeerks would die almost instantly.

<Prince Alloran, we can't just kill them all,> I said. I looked closely at him to see if maybe he had been joking.

His eyes were cold. <*Aristh* Elfangor, I give the orders. You obey the orders.>

<But they're helpless,> I protested.

<They are Yeerks. And this is war. Would you rather wait till they have Taxxon bodies?>

I didn't know what to say. I looked at Arbron. He kept his face carefully expressionless.

<We . . . we can't do this,> I said. <It's wrong. They are our prisoners. We can't! It would be murder!>

<Be careful what you accuse me of, *Aristh* Elfangor,> Alloran said harshly. <You're a child, so I forgive your impertinence. This time. But you are here to learn, not to question orders. And one of the things you'll learn, my idealistic *aristh,* is that war is not about striking brave poses and playing the hero. War is about killing.>

<Andalites do not kill prisoners,> I said.

Alloran laughed. <Is that what they taught you in school?> He laughed again. <Well, child, I learned my lessons in the battle for the Hork-Bajir world, not in a classroom. And let me tell you: The only thing that matters is staying alive. Besides, little *aristh* Elfangor, it's a bit late for you to get delicate. Not now, with the blood of your enemies staining your tail.>

This wasn't happening. It couldn't be. Alloran was a war-prince. I couldn't disobey a war-prince. But this was monstrous.

<I won't kill prisoners,> I said. <Not even Yeerks.>

<I could execute you right now for disobeying me,> Alloran said.

For a moment that seemed to stretch on and on, we stood there, face-to-face. I could barely breathe. I was risking my life, and probably destroying my future in the military, just to save my enemies. It was insane!

But I could not imagine myself sending the Yeerks flying off into the vacuum of space. I couldn't do it.

<Sir,> Arbron said tentatively. <We are so close to the planet surface that Yeerk sensors might pick up the heat signature of thousands of Yeerks being . . . flushed . . . into space. And they would investigate.>

It was true. Maybe. But was it enough to get the prince to back off?

<Well, we wouldn't want that,> Alloran said sarcastically. <We'll wait till we've completed our mission on the surface. Then, as we leave the system, we'll clean out this filth.>

I breathed again. But I wasn't fooling myself. I had made an enemy of Prince Alloran. And I wasn't sure I could count on Arbron, either.

<Time to acquire the Taxxons, if that meets with *Aristh* Elfangor's high moral code,> Alloran said.

I turned away and walked back to the two stunned Taxxons. Without hesitating, I placed my hand on one of the Taxxons' slimy flesh.

Morphing technology allows a person to absorb the DNA of any creature he touches. It takes concentration and focus, because the biotechnology of morphing is triggered by thought commands.

Focus, I told myself. *Put everything else out of your mind, and let the Taxxon become a part of you.*

And as I stood there, the Taxxon's DNA migrated into me.

My life, which had gone rapidly downhill at a shocking speed, was about to get much worse.

And then, with the skeptical eyes of Prince Alloran and the frightened stare of Arbron upon me, I began to morph.

chapter 13

As an Andalite <u>aristh</u>, I'd been trained in morphing. Back at basic training they first transformed us with the morphing technology. And they gave us a *djabala* to acquire and morph.

A *djabala* is a small, six-legged animal, maybe a third the size of a young Andalite. It has a mouth and a tail and no natural weapons. It lives by climbing trees and eating the highest leaves.

You have to morph the *djabala* in order to pass the morphing proficiency test. So I did. But then, like a lot of *arisths,* I morphed a *kafit* bird. I have heard that some planets have many types of bird. But since we only have three, and since the *kafit* is the best species of the three, it's popular with young cadets looking for fun.

It was a wonderful experience. I always loved the idea of flying. But of course, morphing for pleasure is discouraged. So I only did it one time.

That was all the morphing I had done. A *djabala* and a *kafit* bird. I had never even dreamed of morphing a Taxxon.

Taxxons are a nauseating species. Even if you've seen holograms of them. But trust me, till you've been up close to a Taxxon, you just don't know how awful they are. The smell alone is enough to make you sick.

But now I had no choice. I had to show Alloran that I was still a good soldier. I had to prove that I was brave, no matter what he thought of me. I couldn't show any hesitation.

So I focused my mind on becoming the Taxxon. And the changes began immediately.

I felt my upper torso begin to melt down into my lower body. As I watched, my blue-and-tan fur ceased being individual hairs and melted into a plasticlike covering. The bare flesh on my upper body did the same thing, turning hard and shiny.

I felt myself falling as my legs shrank. They seemed to be sucked up into my body. Way too fast!

My stomach hit the deck so hard it knocked the air out of me.

Then, almost as quickly, I was lifted back up off the deck. Dozens of sharp cones were sprouting from my belly. I was growing Taxxon legs.

I looked backward through my stalk eyes and saw that my body was stretching out behind me. I was rapidly becoming a fat worm. Ten feet of rippling, slimy segments rolled backward, engulfing my tail. The process made a sound like wet cloth being dragged over gravel.

I could hear my own internal organs dissolving. Squishing, slippery sounds. I could hear other organs, organs I didn't even have a name for, take their place.

Then . . . I was blind!

My eyes had all been blinded at once. I couldn't see anything. I felt fear grow within me. Fear that threatened to become panic. I was blind!

Muddy at first, then sharper, my sight slowly returned. But it didn't exactly make me feel better. It was an eerie, distorted, broken world I saw.

Taxxons have compound eyes. Each red globule eye is really a thousand smaller eyeballs, each one taking its own tiny picture of the world. Everything I saw around me was shattered into a million small frames. It was overwhelming.

And then I felt something new. A new sense . . .

I moved unfamiliar muscles and realized that they operated my mouth. My round, red mouth. And through that mouth came a deluge of sensory input. It was like smell. And like something I'd never really experienced before. It's called the sense of taste, I think.

And what I tasted . . . what I smelled . . . all that my senses cared about was the bright smell of blood.

I never even felt the Taxxon's instincts well up beneath my own troubled and battered Andalite mind. I had no warning. All at once, the Taxxon was in my head.

How can I even convey the horror?

Have you ever felt in yourself some awful, evil urge? Some fugitive thought that you quickly snuffed out? Well, as I became fully Taxxon, I felt such a feeling. And it was not some faint wisp of thought, but a raging, screaming hunger.

A hunger for anything living.

A hunger for anything with a beating heart.

My shattered Taxxon eyes saw two Andalites.

My own people! I wanted to devour my own people.

But Taxxons are not fools. My Taxxon brain saw and understood the Andalite tails. It knew they were weapons. It knew it could not fight them. And that weakness gave rise to a rage that was like a nuclear fire in me.

I was hungry! Hunger like no hunger any other creature can ever know.

As I struggled to reassert my own identity, I understood why the Taxxons had made their alliance with the Yeerks.

The Yeerks had weapons. Weapons to use to feed fresh, warm flesh to the raging Taxxon hunger.

The Taxxons had given up their freedom. But

freedom is nothing to a Taxxon, compared with that hunger.

<How are you doing, Elfangor?> Arbron asked me.

<Fine,> I lied. <Only . . .>

<What?>

<When you morph, be very careful. Be strong. You'll have to fight the hunger.>

Arbron laughed. <What, are you afraid I'm gonna morph and try to eat you?>

<Yes, Arbron. I am afraid.>

chapter 14

The hunger never went away. Even as we spiraled down toward the Taxxon home world, I felt it. I was thankful Loren was safe back in the *Jahar*. I don't know if I could have resisted the Taxxon's appetite.

I really don't know.

As we came in for a landing, ground control appeared on our screens and demanded our clearance. Our ship's computer responded automatically.

Ground control told us they were backed up on off-loading cargo. It would be half a day before they could unload the Yeerks in our hold.

I didn't know how to feel about that. I didn't want thousands of Yeerks to make it safely to their destination. But I didn't want to slaughter them, either. And I had no doubt: If we got away again in the Yeerk ship, Alloran meant to kill the Yeerks in the hold.

The spaceport was a large facility, obviously still under construction. As we came in low for a landing, descending through orange-and-green acid clouds, we could see dozens of other ships resting in their cradles on the ground. Hundreds of Taxxons and Gedds and even Hork-Bajir were busy building, adding new capacity.

But even amidst all the activity, we could spot the Skrit Na raider ship. That was our target. If we were right, the Time Matrix was aboard that ship.

A landing beam guided us to a cradle on the far edge of the facility. We were more than a mile away from the Skrit Na ship. A mile isn't much in space. But on the ground, on an enemy planet, in a body that makes you want to scream, it's a very, very long distance.

<Whatever you do, remember what you are,> Alloran instructed. <You're Taxxons, on a Taxxon planet. Act like it.>

The three of us, in Taxxon morph, exited out the hatch and into the air of the Taxxon home world.

The first thing I noticed was that the sky was a pale gray-brown. The color of dust. The bright clouds were too high up even to be seen. The second thing I noticed was the smell. Everywhere, warm, living hearts were beating. Hork-Bajir hearts. Gedd hearts. Taxxon hearts. Blood rushed through veins. . . .

The spaceport was a vast array of ship-cradles in a dozen different sizes and shapes. Some were taller than ten tall trees. Some lay almost flat, rising just a few feet from the dirt. Some were empty, but most held ships.

There were slow transports unloading cargo, fighters in for repairs, even a gigantic Yeerk Pool ship. I could see the three spider legs of the Pool ship towering over the cradle. There were shredder burns and one of the "legs" was shattered. The ship had been in a battle.

Below the maze of cradles was bare, orange-red dirt. Not a blade of grass, just dirt. There were primitive magnetic levitation rails running through the massive forest of cradles. Train cars, some open, some enclosed bubbles, raced back and forth along the tracks.

Cargo was being loaded onto the train cars by Gedds. The Gedds were the Yeerks' first victims. The first race they enslaved. Gedds almost seem to walk on two legs, like humans, but they are actually always hunched over so that they can keep one hand on the ground for balance.

We took an open elevator from the cradle down to the ground. As we descended, I counted two ships landing and one taking off. The mag-lev trains zipped back and forth on the dizzying array of tracks. On the ground, big tracked vehicles moved heavier loads.

Everywhere were Taxxons, swaggering Hork-Bajir, and busy, clumsy Gedds. Each was a Controller. A slave to the Yeerk in its head.

It was a huge, raucous, noisy place, full of steel and dust and the smells of solvents and Taxxon filth.

<Busy,> Alloran muttered. <Awfully busy.>

I knew what he meant. Back home, they'd told us the Yeerks were being stopped by our forces. The average Andalite civilian thought we were beating the Yeerks. But this spaceport was evidence to the contrary. The spaceport, just one of several on this one planet, was alive with hurried activity.

Suddenly . . .

"Sssnnnrreewaaaaaa!"

I looked up just in time to see a Taxxon slip from the mag-lev train track overhead. He hit the ground like a bag of goo. His needle legs crumpled and his worm body split open.

It was pandemonium! Taxxons came rushing from all sides.

WHUMPF! A big Taxxon slammed into me, practically knocking me over. More of them, all rushing, came toward their fallen friend.

But they were not rushing to help.

They were rushing to eat the still-living Taxxon.

Then I felt the hunger. It swept me up. I couldn't resist. I was moving forward, jostling to get at the screaming worm myself! Rushing, pushing, shoving, desperate to reach him and . . . and . . .

NO!

I felt my own mind snap back to the surface. It had been overwhelmed by the Taxxon's own instincts. But even now, even with all my willpower, I couldn't resist!

It was as if I were being drawn by a magnet. As if I were being sucked into a black hole. The smell of the wounded Taxxon, the fevered beating of its heart, the . . .

NO!

I was there. *There*, looking down at the injured Taxxon through my shattering compound eyes. I plunged my upper body downward, mouth open, teeth gnashing, ready to . . .

NO! NO! I pulled back. But the power of that hunger would not release me.

I motored my dozens of cone legs, pulling back, and the other, eager Taxxons pushed me aside, heedless.

Where were Arbron and Alloran?

I'd lost them in my mad rush to feed.

I pulled back and back farther, each step like moving a million pounds. And yet I did move away. The feeding frenzy became ever more nightmarish. Taxxons crawled over each other to get at the fresh meat.

I managed to turn my huge, long worm body around and ran from it. I ran as fast as the Taxxon limbs would carry me.

I found a shaded spot under one of the towering ship-cradles and I cowered there, using all my strength to resist. Finally, after a while, the frenzy passed. Not because I had grown strong. But simply because I could now smell that there was no more meat left.

The Taxxon horde broke up and slithered off in various directions, back to their work. Where was Arbron? Where was Prince Alloran?

I was lost and alone on the Taxxon world.

All I could think of doing was heading toward the Skrit Na ship. Hopefully, my two fellow Andalites would be there.

I had to remind myself that we had a mission: the Time Matrix. If the Yeerks realized what was in that Skrit Na ship, there would be no hope at all.

Then, although the image was fractured, I saw Hork-Bajir coming toward me. Six or seven of them, moving in swiftly. Surrounding me!

There was nothing I could do. I couldn't run. A ten-foot-long worm does not outrun a Hork-Bajir.

One Hork-Bajir-Controller swaggered up before me. At a signal from him, the others all leveled Dracon beams straight at me. Not that they needed

Dracon beams. A Hork-Bajir can slice a Taxxon to ribbons in seconds.

And I had seen what happened to any Taxxon careless enough to be injured.

"Welcome to the Taxxon home world," the Hork-Bajir said. "I am Sub-Visser Seven. You interest me. Yes, indeed. I am very interested in any Taxxon who will not eat fresh meat."

chapter 15

Morphing power is a wonderful tool. It allows Andalites to pass among many different species. It makes us the greatest spies in the galaxy.

But it has an awful drawback. You see, if you stay more than two hours in morph, you stay there forever. You become a *nothlit.* An Andalite living out his life in a different body.

That was my greatest fear as the Hork-Bajir-Controllers led me to a mag-lev train car. The sub-visser commandeered the train car. He ordered everyone else off. I stood there, helpless, surrounded, as the mag-lev car shot away from the platform.

It wound its way through the maze of ship-cradles, through the construction workers who were busy building up the might of the Yeerk Empire.

The Yeerk sub-visser said nothing. He seemed almost bored. He slouched his Hork-Bajir body and watched the passing sights gloomily.

I watched him as well as I could with my Taxxon eyes. A sub-visser is a high rank. I remembered that from the basic training classes where they taught us about the Yeerk foe. At the top of the Yeerk Empire is the Council of Thirteen. One of those thirteen is emperor, but no one knows which one. It's a closely guarded secret. The Yeerks fear assassination.

Just below the Council of Thirteen are the vissers. They are the generals of the Yeerk military. They are numbered according to their power and importance. Visser One would be the most powerful, on down through Visser Forty or so.

A sub-visser is like a colonel. Very powerful, especially if he has a low number like seven. But not a visser yet.

The sub-visser spoke. "So, Andalite, how long have you been in this morph?"

I had to stop myself from crying aloud. He knew! He knew I was an Andalite.

No . . . wait. Maybe he didn't know. Maybe he was trying to trick me.

"Ssssewwaari ssstwweeeshh," I said. I didn't know what it meant. The Taxxon body had Taxxon instincts, but not a Taxxon's life learning. So I couldn't speak the Taxxon language. But maybe the sub-visser couldn't, either. He'd been speaking *Galard* so far — the language of interstellar trade and commerce. It was the language many races had learned, back when the galaxy was at peace. It was used to communicate between different species.

The sub-visser looked at me with his slitted

Hork-Bajir eyes. "Don't waste that snake-speak on me. If you're one of us, you'll be able to speak *Galard.*"

Was this another trap? Could Taxxon-Controllers speak *Galard*? Was it even possible for them, with their strange mouths? I didn't know. I had no experience speaking with sounds. And even though I still had the translator chip in my head, it could not interface with my Taxxon brain. What could I do?

The sub-visser laughed. "So. You want to resist me? Good. I need the entertainment. It's rather dull, being in charge of security for this sector. I suppose you're one of the rebels. One of those mountain Taxxons who refuse to join the Empire. Well, we'll get to the truth quickly enough."

Mountain Taxxons? Rebels? I was so surprised I temporarily forgot to be terrified. There were still Taxxons resisting the Yeerks? This would be huge news to my people. We'd assumed all the Taxxons had accepted Yeerk rule in exchange for promises of fresh, unusual meats.

The train car was riding a hundred feet off the dismal plain now, just getting beyond the outskirts of the spaceport. Through the window I could actually see the cradled Skrit Na ship as we zipped past.

I hoped Alloran and Arbron had made it there. I hoped they would complete the mission. Because it didn't look as if I would be there to help them.

Then, suddenly, the train car veered sharply left and I saw a mound, almost a small mountain. It was maybe two or three hundred feet high. Nothing but a slag-heap of dirt excavated from the construction of ship-cradles, really.

But it seethed.

There were holes everywhere, holes the size of a Taxxon. Taxxons were crawling in and out of the holes. Their pulsating worm bodies would slither and wallow into the mound. Others would emerge, seeming to almost blink with their foul red mouths.

"Rebels are just fresh meat," Sub-Visser Seven said calmly. "But being a Taxxon, you understand. Any rebels we catch go to feed loyal Taxxons. It's sad, really. But I have no choice. It's one of the idiotic regulations I have to deal with. It's all part of our deal with the Taxxons: Any suspect Taxxon is turned over to loyal Taxxons for interrogation. Of course, Taxxons don't really interrogate. They don't have the patience for it. They ask one or two questions, then . . . well, then it's dinnertime."

I must have quivered in terror. The sub-visser grinned a Hork-Bajir grin. "Of course, you could tell me why you're here, and what your mission really is . . . *Andalite*. You'll still be executed, of course. But I can make it painless. Much better than being eaten alive."

He did know what I was! He'd been toying with

me. He knew I was an Andalite. But I sensed he was telling the truth: I could either confess and demorph, or die the death the Taxxon-Controllers would inflict.

This is what it had come to. All my hopes of being a great hero. It all ended here, just this quickly.

I felt sick down to my bones. How had everything gone so horribly wrong?

But I couldn't tell the Yeerks anything. The *Jahar* was still up in orbit. If I confessed, the two humans would be taken by the Yeerks. Alloran and Arbron, who were probably still free, might be caught, too.

And there was the Time Matrix. The Time Matrix sat unnoticed in a Skrit Na ship, just a mile from where we stood. And that could mean the end of all Andalites.

I couldn't talk. I *couldn't.*

The sub-visser leaned close to me. He actually whispered. "There is one other possibility. This Hork-Bajir body I use is fine, but there are millions of Hork-Bajir-Controllers now. And what are my other choices? To go back to being a Gedd? Or to take a Taxxon body? No thanks. I won't live with that Taxxon hunger."

The train plunged into the Taxxon hive. Darkness descended. In the darkness, my Taxxon eyes actually worked better.

The sub-visser's Hork-Bajir face was a shattered

sparkling of tiny images to my Taxxon eyes. I could hear his heart beating faster.

"There is one other possibility, Andalite. There has never been an Andalite-Controller. None of us has ever succeeded in capturing an Andalite alive. Your warriors use that nasty Andalite tail blade on themselves rather than be taken alive." He grinned. "Such a waste. Really. See, I want to be the first to have an Andalite body. With that body, with the Andalite morphing power, I wouldn't remain a sub-visser for long. I could be a full visser."

An Andalite-Controller? This Yeerk scum wanted to take over an Andalite body?

I felt a wave of revulsion. A wave of revulsion that seemed to grow out of some deep insight, as if I had caught a glimpse of the future. I wasn't a mystic. I was in the military. But still, I felt a weird, unsettling sensation.

I looked at the sub-visser. I looked into his greedy, murderous eyes. And it was as if I could see him clearly. As if the veil of time was lifted.

And I knew then I would not die. Not yet, at least. I knew it deep in my heart. Because I knew that in looking at this creature, this Yeerk, I was looking at my true, personal enemy.

"Let me take that Andalite body," he said. "You'll live. It's the *only* way you'll live."

<My name is Elfangor, Yeerk,> I said. <Remem-

ber the name. You'll be hearing it again. But you will never take me alive.>

"A pity," the Yeerk sneered. "Stop the car!" he yelled to his Hork-Bajir. "Open the door."

The mag-lev train stopped smoothly. The door opened.

We were on a track deep inside the Taxxon hive. There was a large, open cavern around us, as if the hive was hollow at its core. And down below, perhaps twenty feet down, there was a seething mass of Taxxons.

"See them?" the sub-visser asked. "Taxxons. Not Yeerks. No, those are Taxxons in their natural state. Unimproved, you might say. As savage and bloodthirsty as any creature in the galaxy."

The Taxxons below spotted us above them. They raised their eternally hungry red mouths up to gape at us. They knew what was going to happen next.

The Hork-Bajir surrounded me. I wanted to fight, but I had no weapons. There was nothing I could do.

"Throw him out," the sub-visser said.

The Hork-Bajir rushed at me. They pushed my sagging, flaccid flesh. I scrabbled desperately with my rows of cone legs, but it was useless. They rolled and shoved and slid me, helpless, to the door.

And then I was falling . . .

chapter 16

Falling . . .

<Demorph!> I screamed at myself.

Even as I was falling, I was demorphing. If I was going to die, I'd die an Andalite, not some disgusting, cannibalistic worm.

WHUUUMMMMPPPFFF!

I hit the ground. I hit it hard. The sides of my Taxxon body burst open from the impact. And in a flash, the other Taxxons were on me.

<Demorph!>

But I couldn't possibly morph quickly enough. Red Taxxon mouths drew back and rose up high, plunging straight down into my shattered flesh.

The pain of the fall had been dulled by sheer shock. But this pain . . . *this* pain I felt. I have never known anything so terrible. In my darkest nightmare I've never even imagined . . .

<Ahhhhhhhhh!> I screamed. But just as loudly, I screamed, <Demorph!>

It was a race. A race to see whether I would die before I could demorph. Again and again they ripped at me. But now my Taxxon flesh was shrinking away from them. It was changing. Becoming some strange, new meat.

It would all depend on how the morph happened. If my head emerged too soon, the Taxxons would simply rip it off. I didn't need my head. I didn't even need my legs.

I needed my tail.

If any Andalite in all of history needed his tail, I needed mine. Right NOW!

<Ahhhhhhhhhh!> The pain was unbearable. I was delirious, unable even to think, to focus, to keep track of what was happening to me.

It wasn't going to work! I had been wrong to hope. Wrong to imagine I could survive.

But then . . . I felt some distant part of me move.

And I sensed a shudder pass through the ravenous Taxxons.

With what was left of my Taxxon eyes, I saw it appear . . . all the way back at the end of my Taxxon body.

A bright blade! My tail!

I slashed! Missed!

But it made the Taxxons back away. And while they were reconsidering, my legs grew long and strong. The last of my bleeding worm body shrank and hardened. I heard bones growing inside me.

And then I could see. I could see again!

The Taxxons came at me again, rushing at me, bold with hunger. But now the situation had changed.

Oh, yes, the situation had definitely changed.

I aimed, I slashed! I aimed, I slashed! I aimed, I slashed!

<Come on, you filthy worms! Come on! Come ON!>

And suddenly, even the Taxxons had decided they didn't want to eat me. Instead, the Taxxons I had cut were set upon by the rest.

Through my stalk eyes I saw the sub-visser and his Hork-Bajir soldiers looking down and laughing.

The cold voice of the sub-visser said, "Kill him. Shoot the Andalite scum."

The Hork-Bajir soldiers raised their weapons and sighted on me.

TSEEWWW! TSEEWW!

Dracon beams singed the air above me and melted the dirt at my feet. I couldn't outrun them. I had to hide! But hide where?

Oh.

I dove back into the Taxxon feeding frenzy. Their sluggish, sloppy bodies pressed in all around me. It was sickening, but it gave me cover.

"Go in after him," the sub-visser ordered. "Cut him to pieces!"

Six huge Hork-Bajir leaped down from the train

track. There was no way I could defeat six Hork-Bajir warriors. I was exhausted, on the edge of collapse.

But there was one last desperate hope. The *kafit* bird.

Once you do a morph, the DNA stays with you. Once you've morphed a creature, you can morph it again. And I needed wings as much as I'd needed my tail.

I squirmed between the huge worms, keeping away from their mouths. Not that they wanted to fight an Andalite right then.

And as I felt the Taxxon flesh pressing in around me — smothering me, but at the same time hiding me from the Hork-Bajir — I morphed again. I shrank. I grew smaller and smaller.

"Back, you Taxxon *hogren kalach*!" the Hork-Bajir yelled in a mix of *Galard* and the Hork-Bajir language.

The Taxxons began to pull away, driven back by slashing Hork-Bajir wrists and elbows. I was in the open. A Hork-Bajir was standing over me. He was looking right down at me.

Had I finished morphing?

No time to worry. I would either fly . . . or die.

I opened what I hoped were my six pairs of *kafit* wings. I spread them wide. I flapped hard.

And I flew.

Up off the ground. Up from the dirt. I flew!

I flew inches above the Hork-Bajir. I flew over the sub-visser, who was now screaming in rage at his soldiers. "Shoot it! Shoot it!"

"But the Taxxons may be hit!" one of the Hork-Bajir protested.

"I really don't care, shoot! Shoot! Kill it! SHOOOOOT!"

But it was too late. I was in the air. I raced as fast as my wings would take me, back down the stinking tunnel toward daylight. I saw the brown-gray light ahead, and I flew toward it as if my life depended on it.

I exploded from the tunnel into the open with the outraged cries of the sub-visser ringing in my ears.

<I made it!> I cried to no one but myself. <I made it! I'm alive!>

I flew at the *kafit* bird's top speed back toward the spaceport. Somewhere back there were Alloran and Arbron. Somewhere back there the Time Matrix still waited to be discovered. There was still a mission and the hope of returning safe and alive to the *Jahar*.

And . . . there was life. Life! Life never feels so sweet as when you've come right up against death.

Then I saw it.

It was descending the last few feet into a large

ship-cradle. It was unlike any other craft at the spaceport. Unlike anything any Yeerk had ever designed or built.

The *Jahar*!

The *Jahar* was landing.

It was impossible! There was no one aboard the *Jahar* but the two humans. How could it be landing? *Why* was it landing?

I soared as high as I could and saw that Yeerks in all shapes and sizes were rushing to meet the amazing ship.

They clustered around, many with weapons drawn. Looking back, I saw a mag-lev train come tearing at top speed from the Taxxon mound. I knew in my heart that Sub-Visser Seven was on that train.

It took several minutes for the docking clamps to be fitted to the alien craft. And more minutes while the Yeerks trained every weapon they had on the one small ship.

The mag-lev train arrived, slamming carelessly into two slow-moving Gedds. Out stepped Sub-Visser Seven. He had only four of his original six Hork-Bajir with him. I guess the other two had paid the ultimate price for failing their commander.

The hatch of the *Jahar* appeared. It opened, and out stepped a creature no Yeerk had ever seen before.

It walked on only two legs.

It held up its hands, and said, "Hey, hey. Relax. You can put down the weapons. I'm not here to fight. I'm here to trade."

Chapman!

He realized that the Yeerks did not understand him. So with his hands he pretended to be handing them something, and then receiving something from them.

Sub-Visser Seven strutted to meet the alien. He laughed cynically. "It wants to trade," he said. "This strange creature wants to trade. So. What do you have to trade, alien?"

Neither Sub-Visser Seven nor Chapman had understood a word the other had said. And yet, they understood each other perfectly.

Chapman kept his hands raised and made a human smile. Then, very slowly, he stepped back into the shadowed interior of the ship. And when he reappeared, he was shoving someone before him.

It was Loren. She was bound with wire. Chapman pushed her viciously. She fell to the ground before Sub-Visser Seven.

"That's what I have to trade," Chapman said. "A whole planet full of . . . *that.*"

<You have a plan?>
<Sure,> I said.<We bluff. We tell those Gedd-Controllers up there that we've come to fix the computers. Then we fly that sorry Skrit Na ship away.>

I wanted to sound casual. Nonchalant. The way the fighter pilots always sound when they are describing some terrifying battle. Like it was all no big deal.

Arbron stared at me through red jelly Taxxon eyes. <Okay. Lead the way,> he said.

Arbron and I slithered out from beneath the ship cradle and motored our rows of Taxxon needle-legs up the ramp to the ship itself. Just a pair of bored Taxxon technicians going to work. Totally calm.

Or as calm as any Taxxon, even a Taxxon-Controller, can ever be. There is simply no way to explain the awful hunger of the Taxxon. It is beyond any hunger you've ever imagined. It is constant. Like a screaming voice in your head. Screaming so loud you can't think.

Every living thing you see or smell is just meat to you. You hear beating hearts and smell rushing blood and the hunger almost takes over your body.

And when someone is injured . . . when there is blood spilled . . . well then, as I knew personally, the hunger is all but impossible to resist.

I had come within a haunch hair of eating an injured Taxxon myself. Not something I wanted to remember. But not something I'd ever forget.

<Don't hesitate,> I advised Arbron as several Gedds turned to blink curiously at us. <Look like you're on your way to work.>

<Shut up, Elfangor,> Arbron said harshly.

Again I felt the chill of fear. Something was horribly wrong. But there was no stopping now. I pushed rudely past a Gedd who was in my way.

The Gedd-Controllers looked resentful. But they had no reason to suspect us. We were Taxxons. They had to assume we were Taxxon-Controllers. We looked like we were there to work. No reason for them to be at all suspicious.

Except that one of them was.

One of the Gedd-Controllers stood right in front of us, seemingly unimpressed. He spoke in Galard, the language of interstellar trade. It sounded hard on his Gedd tongue, but I could understand him.

"Rrr-what arrrre you doing herrrrrre?"

If it was hard for the Gedd to make Galard sounds, it was almost impossible for me, with a Taxxon's mouth and tongue. But I couldn't use thought-speak. I might as well announce that I was Andalite. I had to try to speak Galard with a three-foot-long Taxxon tongue.

So I tried. "Sreeeee snwwweeeyiiir sreeeyah!"

Which was not even close to being the sounds I'd wanted to make. What I had meant to say was "computer repair." But the Taxxon's tongue is so long, that it would be hard even if I was used to using a mouth to make sounds.

The Gedd stared at me with its tiny yellow eyes. "Rrr-use rrr pad!" He pointed furiously down at a small computer pad attached to his wrist.

<It's some kind of translator,> Abron said. <Some primitive version of our own translator chips. Let me do it.>

He reached with one of his weak, two-fingered Taxxon hands and pressed several buttons. From the pad came a disembodied voice, speaking Galard.

"Computer repair."

The Gedd snorted angrily. "Rrryou Taxxon wearrrers think you rrrown the planet! Arrrogant as Horrrk-Bajir!"

Abron and I shoved past him into the Skrit Na ship. Unfortunately, it was so cramped and low that we could barely drag our massive bodies inside.

The bridge of the Skrit Na ship was identical to the Skrit Na ship we'd boarded to rescue the two humans. There were two cocooned Skrit glued into a corner. They wouldn't cause any trouble. They didn't look ready to hatch into Na just yet. And there was an active Skrit, what Loren had described as a giant cockroach, scurrying around almost brain-lessly, polishing and cleaning.

There were no Na that I could see. Aside from the Skrit, the bridge of the ship was empty.

<So far, so good,> I muttered. <I'm going to close the hatch. We'll demorph, power up, and be off-planet before they know what's hit them.>

<Yeah. Okay,> Arbron said. <Ready?>

<Yep.> I focused on my breathing, trying to fight the raging Taxxon hunger and my own fear. <Okay, do it!>

Arbron punched the pad to close the hatch door. It slid shut and made a snug vacuum seal *shwoomp*!

I focused all my thoughts on demorphing. I wanted out of that Taxxon body. The two of us could barely move in the cramped bridge, let alone fly the ship. The idiot Skrit kept banging against me, unable to find a way to go around.

I demorphed. I shed that vile Taxxon body as fast as I could. I felt the awful hunger weaken and my own Andalite mind rise above, freed of the Taxxon's instincts.

THUMP! THUMP! THUMP!

The Gedds were pounding on the hull. "Rrrrwhat arrrre you doing? Open rrrup!"

I ignored the noise and punched the engine power. The main engines began to whine as they powered up.

And then I realized it. Arbron was not demorphing.

<Arbron, what are you waiting for? Demorph!>

Arbron didn't say anything.

Thump! Thump! Thump!

"Rrrr-open up! Powerrrr down rrryou fool!"

<Arbron! What are you up to? Demorph!> I yelled. I guess I hoped that yelling would make it happen. But I already knew. He stared at me through those shimmering, red jelly eyes, and I knew. More quietly, almost begging, I said, <Come on, Arbron. Demorph.>

<I really wish I could, Elfangor,> he said. <I really wish I could.>